GETTING EVEN WITH DAD

GETTING EVEN WITH DAD

A NOVELIZATION BY ELIZABETH FAUCHER
BASED ON THE SCREENPLAY WRITTEN BY
TOM S. PARKER & JIM JENNEWEIN

SCHOLASTIC INC.
New York Toronto London Auckland Sydney

MACAULAY CULKIN   TED DANSON

GETTING EVEN WITH DAD

METRO-GOLDWYN-MAYER Presents a JACOBS/GARDNER Production a HOWARD DEUTCH Film
MACAULAY CULKIN TED DANSON "GETTING EVEN WITH DAD"
GLENNE HEADLY SAUL RUBINEK GAILARD SARTAIN and HECTOR ELIZONDO Editor RICHARD HALSEY Production Designer VIRGINIA L. RANDOLPH Director of Photography TIM SUHRSTEDT
Executive Producers RICHARD HASHIMOTO Written by TOM S. PARKER & JIM JENNEWEIN Produced by KATIE JACOBS and PIERCE GARDNER Directed by HOWARD DEUTCH

No part of this publication may be reproduced in whole or in part, or stored in a retrieval system, or transmitted in any form or by any means, electronic, mechanical, photocopying, recording, or otherwise, without written permission of the publisher. For information regarding permission, write to Scholastic Inc., 555 Broadway, New York, NY 10012.

ISBN 0-590-48263-7

12 11 10 9 8 7 6 5 4 3 2 1   4 5 6 7 8 9/9

Printed in the U.S.A.   01

First Scholastic printing, July 1994

GETTING EVEN WITH DAD

Chapter 1

The rare coin was absolutely beautiful. It was a 1920-S Saint-Gaudens twenty-dollar gold piece, and it was worth *forty thousand* dollars. People looking at the coin would find it hard to believe that something so small could be so incredibly valuable.

And some of those people would find the idea of *stealing* it almost impossible to resist.

Of course, behind the heavily guarded doors at the Certified Coin Grading Service in San Francisco, no one had any disloyal thoughts of that sort at all. The coin graders — many of them elderly, *all* of them wearing white gloves — sat hunched at their desks in complete silence, studying coins through special magnifiers. The office was somehow both cavernous and claustrophobic, and the footsteps of the many armed guards echoed ominously as they patrolled the facility, twenty-four hours a day.

The coin graders rarely spoke, working with slow precision, looking for the microscopic flaws in otherwise perfect coins. They would lift each coin with careful gloved fingers, peer through their magnifiers, and make precise notes in neat, black ink on the ledgers next to them.

The man grading the brilliantly cast Saint-Gaudens twenty-dollar gold piece took his time examining each minute aspect of the coin before writing down his verdict. This information was then transferred to a computer, which printed out: "1920-S $20 SAINT, MS-66 APPRAISED VALUE: $40,000." After lengthy perusal of another coin, he wrote: "1880-O $1 MORGAN, MS-65 APPRAISED VALUE: $20,000." Despite the magnitude of these numbers, he didn't even blink, instead simply moving on to the next coin on his list.

Once the appraisals had been completed, each coin with its printed description was placed in a small, see-through plastic holder, which was then sealed shut. This plastic "slab" would protect the valuable coins from any damage while being handled by prospective buyers, or being transferred elsewhere. The slab was gently placed on a tray with other rare mint-condition gold and silver coins. Once the tray was full, it was picked up by one of the armed guards, who would carry it to the vault to be locked safely away behind heavy steel doors.

These old coins were worth *serious* money.

Down in the street, looking up at the imposing brick building where the coin graders worked, were three people who were *very* interested in the future of those coins. The leader of the group was Ray Gleason, who was tall, and confident, and full of likeable charm. Even with his hair flopping down over his forehead and dressed in flour-dusted work clothes, he looked like a man with a vision. He had had some bad luck over the years but knew that with just *one* good break, he could turn his life around. Working in a bakery was fine, but he dreamed of starting his own confectionary business one day soon.

Unfortunately, this was a very expensive dream.

His partners in crime stood next to him in the street, waiting to hear his plan. Bobbie was dark haired, quick moving, and *constantly* suspicious of everyone and everything. He was so intense that he could almost never stand still, and even now, he shoved his hands in and out of his pockets and shifted his weight from one foot to the other. Bobbie knew that life always had an angle — all he had to do was *find* it.

Carl, who was probably bigger than Ray and Bobbie put together, was a completely different type. Thick in both body and mind, he looked as if he could probably bench-press a Volkswagen bus — or at least a Hyundai. His two obsessions in life were food and clothes. He took tremendous pride in his tailored, if beefy, appearance and always wore a suit and tie. He was also rarely seen without a snack and had taken

advantage of the fact that they were standing near a hot dog cart to buy a foot-long
dog with sauerkraut and everything else
on it. He leaned forward as he ate it, concentrating on trying to keep the dripping
mustard, relish, onions, and sauerkraut
from falling onto his clothes.

"So, picture this," Ray said, automati-
cally falling into the smooth patter of a born
salesman. "This crazy old lady lived alone
down in Fremont. No friends, no relatives.
Day the county buries her, nobody even
shows."

Bobbie nodded intently, while Carl
frowned, troubled by this image, his hot
dog forgotten.

"A couple of days later," Ray went on,
"someone from the state tax office comes
poking around and finds this trunk up in
her attic."

Carl frowned, trying to picture this new
scene, while Bobbie just nodded.

"What's he find?" Ray asked dramati-
cally, and then continued with his story before Carl could reply. A mother lode of
rare coins! *Totally* uncirculated. Like maybe these just came out of the mint." He

shrugged, thinking of plausible reasons to explain why this had happened. "Maybe her husband, who died a while back, had the coins from years ago. Maybe she didn't even know they were there."

Carl started to say something, but Bobbie shook his head impatiently, and Carl subsided, taking a bite of what was left of his sloppy snack.

"So," Ray continued with a grin, "being as there's no relatives or will, the state confiscates them, right? And they're going to sell them, maybe auction them off."

Bobbie and Carl were *both* frowning now, but Bobbie's frown was thoughtful, while Carl's just looked perplexed.

"But, before they do that, these coins have to be appraised," Ray said. "And that happens right here in San Francisco" — he pointed triumphantly up at the big brick building across the street — "at the Certified Coin Grading Service."

Bobbie followed his gaze, also starting to grin.

The building had a construction chute leading from the second floor down to a huge Dumpster in an alley. Two construction workers were standing in an upstairs window, sending broken pieces of old wallboard material down the chute, the pieces landing with heavy thuds. Obviously, part of the building was being renovated. It was also obvious that a lot of different people like workers and contractors and supervisors were going in and out of the building without attracting much attention. All they would have to do to get inside would be to blend in with everyone else.

"They're on the top floor," Ray said, pointing. "Pickups are by armored car from the parking level, between five and six in the afternoon."

Bobbie nodded, already starting to guess the plan, and then they both looked over at Carl to see what he thought. As it turned out, Carl wasn't even paying attention, because he was busy blotting his tie with his handkerchief, looking very worried as he tried to remove a bit of mustard.

Bobbie pushed his arm. "Hey, fashion plate! You got that?"

"Trying to," Carl said, thinking that he meant the spot on his tie. "Trick is to blot. *Never* rub." Then he stopped blotting, not sure why they were looking at him with barely disguised impatience. "This is *silk*," he said plaintively, indicating the tie. "Cost me forty-five bucks."

Ray reached over to straighten the tie, unable to see any spot at all. Despite Carl's size, he was something of a man-child, and Ray had gotten used to treating him in a calm, avuncular way.

"Look, Carl," he said. "We pull this off, you can buy a *thousand* silk ties. You can be the Silk Tie King of San Francisco Bay. But first, you maybe have to pay a little attention here."

Carl thought that over and then nodded. "I hear ya, Ray," he said, neatly folding the handkerchief, putting it in his pocket, and arranging the folds so that just one corner peeked out. "I'm with the program."

"Good," Ray said, and resumed his story, looking up at the top floor of the building with dreamy anticipation. "So, the question is, how much was that poor old widow worth when they lowered her into potter's field?"

None of them knew, but they were all eager to find out.

Chapter 2

The answer to their question came out in
that week's issue of *Numismatist Weekly*.
Ray had managed to find a copy at a very
eclectic newsstand near the university, and
brought it back to his apartment, where he
was meeting Bobbie and Carl. By the time
they arrived, he had already found the article about the poor old widow and circled
the headline in bright red ink. It read:
COIN HORDE FOUND IN TRUNK.

"So?" Bobbie asked, setting several take-
out coffees on the kitchen table and helping
himself to two of them. Carl was already
sitting down and working his way through

the pepperoni pizza they had also brought.

"A million five," Ray said.

Bobbie whistled, and Carl stopped chewing for a few seconds.

"That's seven hundred and fifty grand for us," Ray said, and paused for effect. "A quarter million apiece."

"Who's the fence?" Bobbie asked suspiciously.

"A guy named Dobbs," Ray said, tearing open two sugar packets and pouring them into the remaining cup of coffee before Bobbie could claim it, too. "He's a specialist. Breaks the coins out of their holders, so they can't be traced, and then moves them to dealers in Hong Kong and Europe."

Carl wiped his hands with a napkin and then picked up the newspaper, trying to sound out its name. "Nu-mumis . . . Numisma . . ." He shook his head, and dropped the paper, returning to what was left of the pizza. Then the telephone rang, and he made a move to answer it.

"Don't get that," Ray said quickly. "It's probably Nadine."

The phone rang again and then again.

Carl frowned. "I thought you liked Nadine."

"I *did*," Ray said, "until she brought me that plant." He gestured toward a sickly, yellowing elephant fern that was on the floor in the corner of the dingy kitchen.

The phone rang twice more and then stopped.

"Good," Ray said, and looked back at Carl. "See, when a woman gives you a plant, it's her little way of testing you. Like, if you can take care of it, it's a sign she can move the relationship to the next level, see?"

Carl tilted his head, a little dubious about this theory.

"Believe me," Ray said. "When a woman gives you something you have to water, feed, or take for a walk — it's time to dump her."

Carl looked over at the pathetically withering plant. "Okay, but — I think it's sick."

Ray shrugged. "It dies, it dies."

Carl shook his head sadly. "Glad she didn't give you no cocker spaniel."

*   *   *

Ray and his buddies continued to refine their plan. Ray was still going to work every day to his job at the bakery, and Bobbie and Carl would hang out and watch him as he worked. That is, *Carl* would watch, and Bobbie would pace back and forth and worry a lot.

As Ray put the finishing frosting touches on a magnificent wedding cake, Carl stood next to him, rapt, like a kid in a candy shop. Bobbie just fidgeted with various metal utensils and sent dark scowls in the direction of any other bakery workers who walked within ten feet of them.

"The coin auction is next Wednesday," Ray said, forming a perfect rose out of pink frosting. "They're moving them from the grading service to the auction house on Monday."

Bobbie nodded. "So we grab the stuff while they're moving it." His eyes gleamed as he envisioned the action, holding a spatula out like an **automa**tic weapon. "We hit an **armored car,** and — " He pretended to fire the spatula, making his arms shake from the recoil. "Okay, we'll need *major* firepower. A couple of AK-47s, and — "

Ray cut him off. "*Bob* — we're not invading Iraq. I'd like to do this job *without* wearing a flak jacket, okay? Besides, we'd never find one in Carl's size."

Bobbie glowered and fired a few sulky make-believe rounds from his spatula. He *liked* blowing things up. For that matter, he liked wearing flak jackets.

Ray turned back to his cake just in time to see Carl sampling the frosting. "Carl! Don't poke the cake. You know how long it took me to do this?" Carefully, he squirted out some fresh frosting and smoothed it down, repairing the spot Carl had touched.

Unabashed, Carl licked the frosting off his finger. "You know, Ray," he said thoughtfully. "You're like that guy. That Michael dude, who did that ceiling."

Ray laughed, touching up a yellow rose and an ornate sugary green leaf while he was at it. "That *Michael* dude? You mean, Michelangelo?"

Carl nodded. "But you paint with frosting, man." He gazed at the cake in awe. "And that's *so much* better."

Finished, Ray stepped back and admired

his cake with all the pride of a great artist.

It wasn't half bad — even if he did say so himself.

Out on U.S. 5, the highway running between the town of Redding and the Bay area, a 1983 Cadillac was speeding down the road. Timmy, a bright-eyed eleven-year-old with blond hair, sat alone in the cavernous backseat, sipping a Pepsi and staring out the car window at the scenery whipping by.

Up in the driver's seat, Wayne, who was forty-eight, with thinning hair and a thickening waist, stuffed a double cheeseburger into his mouth, well on his way to thickening even more. Next to him sat Kitty, who was thirty-five, and looked like a cocktail waitress with her teased hair, heavy makeup, and bright red nail polish. Every so often, she sighed prettily and nibbled a few french fries. Then she would check her nails, sigh, and eat some more fries.

Bored beyond belief, Timmy picked up his compact 8mm camcorder, held it at arm's length, aimed it at himself, and turned it on.

"Submitted for your approval," he said in his best Rod Serling voice, pitching it as low as possible. "Sunday, six P.M., lonely stretch of California highway. Timmy Gleason suddenly realizes he's been abducted by alien beings." He made a face of open-mouthed shock and horror at the camera and then leaned over the front seat, sticking the camera in Wayne's face. "The driver says his name is 'Wayne.' But Timmy knows he's really a hideous blob from another galaxy."

Wayne swatted at the camera, trying to knock it aside. "For the last time, get that out of my face! Sit back and be quiet!"

Kitty sighed deeply. "Timmy, honey, do what Wayne says, now."

Timmy sat back against the seat cushions, sullen.

"And you'd better not be spilling anything on my upholstery back there," Wayne said, reaching into the fast-food bag for another double cheeseburger.

Timmy didn't answer. He just continued to stare at the back of Wayne's balding head, and wished for the hundredth time that his aunt Kitty had never married this jerk. He picked up the camcorder again and turned it on, directing it at Wayne's head.

"Sure," he said, "Wayne looked human — right down to his bald spot — but Timmy knew it was all a disguise. No real human being could *ever* eat three double cheeseburgers at one sitting."

Wayne erupted, half-chewed cheeseburger spilling out of his mouth as he reached into the backseat, grabbed for the camera, and missed.

"That does it!" he yelled. "Gimme that camera!"

Since he wasn't looking at the road, the Cadillac swerved into the next lane, nearly hitting another car, which blared its horn.

"Wayne!" Kitty shrieked, covering her eyes with her hands. "Watch out!"

Wayne jerked the wheel back just in time, barely avoiding an accident. As the car skidded toward the shoulder of the road, Timmy was thrown around in the backseat, and his soda went flying. Finally, the Cadillac came to a stop, brakes screeching, tires spewing gravel.

Wayne tried again to grab the camera,

but Timmy scrunched into the corner of the backseat, just out of his reach.

"Gimme that, you little jerk!" Wayne said, making another futile swipe.

Timmy avoided his lunge and kept right on videotaping him. "The alien lashes out, spewing secret sauce — "

Kitty, trying to be the referee, grabbed Wayne's arm. "Wayne, Wayne! Stop it, we're okay." She glared at Timmy. "Shut that camera off!"

Quickly, Timmy shut it off.

"And he spilled soda all over the seat!" Wayne said.

"I know," Kitty said, trying to calm him down. "We'll clean it up, sweetheart. There's a Chevron up ahead. C'mon, honey."

Wayne's hard stare bored into Timmy, but Timmy didn't flinch, as he held the stare defiantly.

"Come *on*, honey," Kitty said.

Wayne broke the stare, put the car into Drive, and headed toward the gas station. He parked near the rest rooms and sat in furious silence as Timmy slowly opened the back door and got out.

"Grab all the paper towels you can get," Kitty said. "Hurry up, now."

Timmy nodded and walked toward the men's room door, his shoulders slumping a little as he listened to Wayne and Kitty argue behind him.

"I *told* you we shouldn't've brought him," Wayne said bitterly.

"Nobody would take him," Kitty answered with a bit of a petulant whine in her voice. "What was I supposed to do with him?"

"I know what *I'd* like to do with him," Wayne said, sounding very grim. "I'd like to drive off and leave him here."

Hearing that, Timmy stopped walking, pausing just outside the men's room door. He didn't want to go *anywhere* with Wayne, but being left alone on a deserted highway, out in the middle of nowhere, would be even *worse*.

Chapter 3

Back in San Francisco, Ray was in his kitchen with Carl and Bobbie. He had the robbery plans spread out on the table while he tried to explain its intricacies to a befuddled Carl. Bobbie stood over by the window, chain-smoking.

"He's never gonna get it," Bobbie said. "Why do we need him, anyway?"

"Because he follows orders," Ray answered. *"Unlike* you." He turned back to Carl. "All right, let me explain this one more time. Remember in high-school science class, the teacher did that little demonstration with the rats in the maze?"

Carl looked at him blankly. He hadn't exactly gotten that far in his scholastic career.

"Well — maybe you were sick that day," Ray said, and ran his hands back through his hair, trying to figure out a simpler approach. "Look, all we're doing is creating a situation where we make the guards go exactly where we want them to go." He used his fingers to walk over the detailed drawings on the plans, demonstrating what he had in mind. "Like — "

Carl's eyes lit up. "Rats in a maze!"

"Right, right!" Ray tapped a spot on the plans. "They end up *here*. We do the grab. Nobody gets hurt, nothing goes wrong."

"Ha," Bobbie said, and lit another cigarette. "That's what you said when we boosted those VCRs."

Since he had heard that complaint a million times, Ray just rolled his eyes.

"I do four years in Folsom for stealing stupid Betamaxes," Bobbie said, waving his cigarette to punctuate the utter waste of his time. "It wouldn't have been half as bad if we got caught with VHS machines — you know, something we could actually *sell.*" He shook his head in disgust. "I mean, even the *judge* laughed at us."

Okay, the incident with the Betamaxes was not Ray's favorite memory. "It was a mistake, okay? And" — Ray paused — "you weren't the only one doing time. Remember that."

Bobbie and Carl exchanged glances, weighing whether it was worth it to risk going to jail *again* for the sake of some dumb *coins*. Of course, the coins were worth a lot more than those Betamaxes.

"Your guy Dobbs, what if he burns us?" Bobbie asked finally.

"He's not going to burn us," Ray said with great confidence. "He's the one who turned me on to the job. I'm telling you, I've got this wired. We walk in, we walk out. Nothing can possibly go wrong."

Just then, there was a knock on the door.

Ray held his finger to his lips, indicating for the other two to be quiet.

There was another knock, this time more insistent.

"Could be Nadine," Carl whispered, looking very worried. "She's going to be upset about her plant, Ray."

Ray signalled for him to shut up, as the knocking turned into outright pounding.

"Ray!" a female voice shouted. "Open up! It's Kitty, your sister!"

Ray blinked, since that was the last person he would have expected to show up at his door. "Kitty?" he said aloud. "What's she — ?"

Kitty slammed her fist against the door a few more times, breaking a nail. "I know you're in there, Ray! Now, open up!"

Swiftly, Ray rolled up the robbery plans and gave them to Bobbie.

"Hide this," he hissed before getting up to go over and open the door.

Bobbie shoved the plans behind a couch cushion and sat in front of it.

Ray put on a big enthusiastic smile and then flung the door open. "Kitty!" he said, beaming. "How you doing? You look great!" He moved to hug her, but she rushed right past him.

"Skip the hugs and kisses, Ray," she said, out of breath. "I don't have much time." Then she noticed Bobbie and Carl. "Who's Rocky and Bullwinkle?"

"Bobbie and Carl, my sister, Kitty," Ray said, by way of an introduction.

Carl always liked to be a gentleman, so he stood up and waved a polite "hi." Bobbie stayed on the couch, blowing out a puff of cigarette smoke and blatantly admiring her legs.

There was an awkward pause, and everyone looked at everyone else.

"So," Ray said heartily. "What're you doing in town? You should've called, told me you were coming."

Kitty frowned at him. "I *did* call. About ten times! But you never answer your phone."

"He thought it was Nadine," Carl explained. "She gave him the plant." He pointed at the withering fern. "Now Ray's all put out 'cause he hates the *big* commitment of watering it once a week."

Ray gritted his teeth, not appreciating the dig. "Would you please go get the lady a beer," he said tightly.

Kitty shook her head. "I don't want a beer. Look. I got married, Ray."

"No *kidding*." Now Ray smiled. "That's great! When?"

A car horn beeped loudly from out in the street, and Kitty looked urgently in the direction of the sound.

"Three hours ago," she said. "And now I'm going on my honeymoon."

Ray nodded and smiled.

"Hi, Dad," Timmy said from the doorway, his voice very tentative.

They all turned to stare at him as he stood there, wearing his backpack and holding his little suitcase with both hands.

Seeing his estranged son, Ray's face fell. Dealing with Timmy was the absolute *last* thing he needed right now.

Bobbie looked from Timmy, to Ray, and back again. *"Dad?!"*

Wanting to save the situation, Kitty pulled Timmy inside the apartment, smoothing down the various cowlicks in his hair and fixing his shirt collar.

"Timmy, now be a good boy and have fun while you're staying with your father," she said, and kissed him, leaving a big lipstick mark on his cheek. "I'll call when I get back, and your dad'll put you on a bus back to Redding, okay?"

Timmy nodded, put his suitcase down,

and rubbed off the lipstick with his shirt sleeve.

Ray held his hands up. "Whoa, Kitty, wait a minute. We gotta *talk*," he said, and ushered her out to the hall, closing the door behind him.

Standing in the kitchen, Timmy looked at Carl and Bobbie curiously.

"So," he said, to break the silence. "You ex-cons, too?"

Carl and Bobbie exchanged measured glances, and then ignored him completely.

Timmy nodded and folded his arms, looking around the ratty apartment without much enthusiasm.

Out in the hall, Ray was doing his best to keep his voice down and sound less frantic than he felt.

"*Seriously* bad timing," he said. "I can't have the kid around right now."

Kitty put her hands on her hips. "Look, Ray, I've had Timmy for three years. *Three years*, Ray — "

Ray nodded, cutting her off. "I know, I know, and I appreciate it, but — "

"So you can take him for a few days," Kitty said.

Not *this* week. "But, I'm telling you," Ray said, his voice rising. "This is a *bad* time for me!"

"And I'm telling you I'M GOING ON MY HONEYMOON!" Kitty yelled.

Outside, Wayne leaned on the car horn again.

"I have to go," Kitty said, hurrying toward the stairs. "Bye, Ray. Make sure he flosses. I'll be home Saturday."

"Wait a minute!" Ray said, chasing after her. "Where you going? Come back! Can't you take him *with* you? Kitty!"

But she was already gone, running down the stairs and slamming the front door of the building as she disappeared outside. Ray stood at the top of the stairs and punched the banister in complete frustration.

It was always hard seeing his son, but this week, it was going to be just plain *impossible*.

Chapter 4

Ray listened as Kitty and her new husband drove away, tires squealing, and then let out his breath. Every problem had a solution, and he just had to figure out how to solve this one. There had to be a way out.

He went back into his apartment, where he could hear Timmy walking around the kitchen and making comments about his lax housekeeping. As Ray started through the living room, Bobbie grabbed his arm.

"Ray, what's with this kid?" he asked angrily. "We can't have him hanging around — "

Ray shook his hand off. "Don't worry. I'll *handle* it."

Exploring the kitchen, Timmy opened the refrigerator. There was nothing on the shelves except for a grapefruit and some gangrenous chicken. It looked disgusting, and he made a face. Hoping that there would be something better to eat in the cupboards, he started opening them, finding almost nothing but mismatched cups and plates, a jar of instant coffee, and a box of stale cereal.

Ray slowly entered the room, trying to decide how he was going to play this. Being cheerfully paternal was probably the best choice, so he put on a breezy demeanor.

"So . . . Timmy," he said. "Tim-bo. Tim-boy." He laughed a little too heartily. "Heh-heh." Breezy wasn't going to work, so he decided to try man-to-man directness. "Look, uh, unfortunately, you've kind of arrived at a — "

Timmy unearthed a dried-out jar of peanut butter and squinted to read the expiration date. " 'June 1989'?" he said, and put the jar down on the counter as though it had burned him. "I think this is expired." He looked around at the rest of the paltry supplies and shook his head. "You'd better make a list."

Ray looked at him without comprehension.

"A shopping list," Timmy elaborated. "I'll need a few things."

He opened his backpack and fished around inside until he came up with a pencil and a spiral notebook. He gave them to Ray, and then walked around the kitchen, grimacing as he inspected the dirty conditions.

"Okay," he said, wiping his hand on his jeans leg after touching the sticky table. "Jif peanut butter, crunchy style. White bread." He glanced at his father. "Don't get rye — I hate rye." Then he thought about what else he might need. "Doritos, Cool Ranch flavor. Pepperidge Farm Double Chocolate Chip cookies." He thought some more. "Count Chocula breakfast cereal. Oreos, Pepsi, and Häagen-Dazs strawberry ice cream." He considered all of that, and then nodded. "Yeah. That should do it for starters."

Ray looked sort of stunned as he stood there holding the unopened notebook.

"Fine," Timmy said, and took the notebook and pencil back. "*I'll* make the list." He started writing, then paused briefly. "Guess I'll be crashing on the couch, right?" he said, and went out to the living room to see if the sofa was going to be fit to sleep on.

Ray finally found his voice and came up for air after being caught in that whirlpool of energy.

"Uh, son," he said uncertainly, "listen — "

He trailed Timmy out to the living room. The boy was bouncing on the couch, testing it, while Bobbie and Carl leaned against the far wall, their expressions grim.

"So, what're we doing this week?" Timmy asked, bouncing. "I heard the aquarium's not bad. 'Course we *have* to go to a Giants game. And I'd like to hit the Museum of Natural History."

"Uh, Timmy," Ray said carefully, avoiding Bobbie and Carl's scowls. "We're not going to be able to — "

Timmy whipped out a folded sheet of paper from his backpack. "I made an itinerary." He looked at Carl, having already figured out that the massive man wasn't exactly an intellectual. "That means a schedule of events."

"Oh," Carl said, and mouthed the word to himself a few times so he might remember it.

Seeing the rolled burglary plans behind one of the couch cushions, Timmy was curious enough to pick them up. "What's this?"

Ray snatched the plans from his hand. "None of your business!"

"What're you so nervous about?" Timmy asked, and then eyed the rolled plans. "You got something to hide?"

All three men immediately shook their heads, protesting their innocence.

"Oh, no, nothing," Ray assured him.

" *Course* not," Bobbie said.

"Uh-uh," Carl agreed. "Nope, nope, nope."

Their response had been so automatic that Timmy, of course, knew that they were lying and looked at them suspiciously.

Realizing that this wasn't going well, Ray looked at Bobbie and Carl.

"Give us a few minutes, will you?" he asked.

Bobbie and Carl went grumbling into the kitchen, leaving Ray and Timmy alone.

His father couldn't seem to think of anything to say, so Timmy spoke first.

"I brought you something, Dad," he said. "A picture of Mom and me." He felt around inside his backpack, and then handed the snapshot to Ray.

In the photograph, Timmy was standing sadly next to a graveyard headstone. Written across the headstone was: BARBARA GLEASON, BORN OCT. 11, 1955, DIED JULY 10, 1989.

Ray stared at the picture, not sure what to say. "I . . . uh — it's . . . nice, Tim. Real nice." He tried to hand it back, but Timmy waved it away.

"Keep it," Timmy said. "I have others." Then he looked his father right in the eye, trying to keep years of anger and hurt inside. "You probably don't get to the grave much, do you?"

Ray didn't say anything.

Timmy nodded abruptly. "Didn't think so." He looked at the yellow fern that Carl had moved over to the window so it would get some sun. "You should water that. It's dying."

"Yeah," Ray said, and put the photograph down on the coffee table. "Sure. Um — I'll do that. Yeah." He sat down on the couch next to his son, trying to take control of this situation. "So. Uh, how're you doing in school?"

Timmy looked at him without blinking. "On my last Stanford Achievement Test, my overall scores rated me in the ninety-fifth percentile."

"No kidding," Ray said, and frowned. "Is that good?"

"It means that intellectually, I'm superior to ninety-five percent of the kids in my class," Timmy said.

Ray looked impressed. "Whoa. That's *great*." Then he searched for something else to ask. "So. You dating yet?"

"I'm *eleven*," Timmy said.

Ray nodded, recovering himself. "Yeah, yeah, it's good to wait. I didn't start dating until I was eleven and a half. Heh-heh-heh."

Timmy just looked at him, not amused.

Not wanting to give up, Ray pressed on. "Well, I'm glad we had this talk," he said. "We should do it more often. But not right now. You see, you picked a bad week to come, Tim. I'm not going to be able to spend any time with you."

Timmy hadn't expected much from his father, but his feelings were still hurt.

"See, I'm really swamped at work right now," Ray said hastily. "At the bakery, you know? I do cakes for them; I design cakes, and we've got a *lot* of cakes this week, so — well, you understand."

Timmy nodded solemnly. If his father was working hard at his job, he wasn't about to discourage that. "Kitty says you learned how to do that in prison," he volunteered. "Make cakes."

Ray was a little nonplussed, but he nodded. "Yeah, yeah, it was kind of a course I took. I *wanted* to get in the counterfeiting class, but it was full up." He looked at Timmy, expecting to get a laugh, but his son didn't even smile.

There was a long silence.

34

"What was prison like?" Timmy asked. "Did you ever try escaping?"

"Escaping," Ray said. "No. No, they kind of frown on that. They've got signs posted and everything."

Again, Timmy didn't smile.

Out in the kitchen, Bobbie and Carl were poised by the door like hunting dogs, eavesdropping as hard as they could.

"Did you get my letters?" Timmy asked.

Ray hesitated, having hoped that his son wouldn't bring that up.

"Why didn't you write back?" Timmy asked, unable to hide how much it had hurt his feelings.

Ray coughed, covering up his discomfort. "I — I guess I didn't have much to say, Tim. I mean, what was I going to write? 'Having a wonderful time, wish you were here'?"

"You never even sent me a *birthday card*," Timmy said accusingly.

Ray got up from the couch, running his hands through his hair, shoving aside his feelings of guilt. He stood there ineptly, then reached into his pocket and dug out a twenty-dollar bill.

"Yeah, yeah, yeah," he said. "Look, I have to discuss a few things with my friends, so here." He tried to give his son the money, but Timmy wouldn't take it. "There's a pizza place on the corner. Go on, get whatever you want."

Timmy looked unhappily at his father. He had had a crazy dream that maybe *this* time would be different and that maybe his father wouldn't push him away. Well, so much for dreams. He grabbed the twenty-dollar bill and started down the hallway instead of toward the front door.

"Hey, where you going?" Ray asked.

Timmy stopped. "If it's not too much to ask, *Dad*," he said sarcastically, "can I use your bathroom?"

Ray sighed, and then nodded. Once Timmy was gone, he went into the kitchen, where Carl was eating the dry peanut butter out of the jar with a bent spoon.

"Don't eat that," Ray said. "It's expired."

Carl frowned, not sure whether to swallow the huge spoonful already in his mouth. Then he shrugged and kept eating.

"Ray, what is this?" Bobbie demanded. "You never told us you had a kid!"

Down the hall, Timmy cracked the door of the bathroom and listened to the conversation.

"So I forgot to tell you," Ray said.

"Well, what are you going to *do* with him?" Bobbie asked. "He gets curious, it could blow this — "

"Don't worry about it," Ray said, with more confidence than he felt. "I'm stuck with him, but we'll work around it. He's just a kid. He has no idea what's going on."

Timmy shut the door, his expression hardening.

His father had *seriously* underestimated him.

Chapter 5

The next morning, when Ray was ready to go to work, Timmy was still asleep on the couch, covered by an old army blanket.

Ray reached down and shook his shoulder gently. "Timmy?"

Timmy woke up and saw his father standing there in his bakery clothes. He flopped back down and stared at the ceiling instead.

"I have to go to work," Ray said. "I left some money there" — he gestured toward a twenty-dollar bill on the coffee table — "in case there's anything you want to pick up at the market." He paused, feeling very guilty. "You going to be okay?"

Timmy didn't answer him, still hurt and upset by what he had overheard the night before.

"Well," Ray took a step away from him. "See you. I'll — be back late."

Timmy turned over on his side, facing away from him.

"Well." Ray bent down and picked up a blue nylon travel bag with a Nike logo, and then opened the door. Before going out into the hall, he turned back to look at the huddled unhappy shape that was his son. "Stay out of trouble," he said, and left.

After the door shut, Timmy, dressed in underwear and a T-shirt, kicked the blanket off. He went over to the window and looked out at the street below.

His father came out of the building, opened the trunk of his car, and tossed the Nike bag in. The way it landed made it look light.

Timmy watched as he drove away, wondering why he was taking a gym bag to work. If his father was the kind of guy who worked out at a health club, that would be one thing, but — he wasn't. Unfortunately, his father *was* the kind of man who sometimes got in over his head. He and his friends were hiding something, and Timmy had a pretty good idea of what it was. He might not know the *details*, but it was a safe bet that his father was up to his old tricks.

Breaking the law.

Timmy turned away from the window and frowned at the dying plant in the corner. Why didn't he just take thirty seconds and *water* the poor thing every so often? If his father couldn't even manage that much, there wasn't much hope that he'd *ever* take the time to love, and take care of, Timmy.

Alone in the apartment, he decided to look around. He walked down the hallway and opened his father's bedroom door, peeking into the disheveled room. The bed was unmade, the shades were crooked, and there was a pile of laundry on the floor. It was a typical bachelor's mess.

It was also the room of a man he didn't know at all. Maybe if he looked at some of his father's possessions, he might find out a little more about him. Maybe he would start to understand him.

Timmy stepped into the room, feeling as if he were trespassing, but too curious to change his mind. He paused in front of the dresser, examining the items on top of it, trying to solve the mystery of who his father was by looking at pieces of his life.

There were a few stray bills — mostly ones, with a couple of fives and tens thrown in. A black comb and a wooden hairbrush sat crookedly next to each other, as though they had been used, and then dropped, in a hurry. There was a battered Elmore Leonard paperback mystery, with what looked like a recipe cut from the newspaper being used as a bookmark. Timmy pulled the bookmark out far enough to see what the recipe was, not surprised to read the ingredients for what seemed to be a very complicated version of seven-layer chocolate cake.

At the back of the dresser there was a dusty jar filled with hundreds of pennies. Next to it was a bottle of cologne, and Timmy unscrewed the top, sniffing the contents. He didn't really like the smell, but he put some on anyway. A hand exerciser was lying discarded behind the penny jar, and Timmy fitted it into his hand. It was too big, but he squeezed the grips a few times, barely managing to move them at all. Touching everything made him feel as if he might be able to get closer to his father, but so far, it wasn't really working.

In front of the mirror, in a cheap plastic frame, was a picture of Ray with his arm around a flashy-looking young woman. They were smiling but still looked as though they each would rather be someplace else, probably with some*one* else.

The picture he had given his father, of him standing next to his mother's gravestone, was face down, near the scattered dollar bills. Timmy looked at it fondly, and then tucked it into the mirror frame so that it would be displayed more prominently. Maybe seeing it would remind his father that he couldn't be dismissed *that* easily.

He stayed in his father's room all morning, playing with things and bouncing around. He set up a wastebasket on top of the dresser, and then wadded up a piece of paper to play an imaginary game of basketball. He jumped on the bed, feigning a dribble with his paper ball and eluding countless NBA defenders.

"Bulls down by one!" he said. "Two seconds left! Pippen drives down the lane. . . ." He took a mighty bounce off the bed toward his wastebasket hoop and slammed the wadded-up paper ball into it. "SLAM DUNK!" he yelled, his momentum knocking the wastebasket off the dresser and scattering the contents all over the floor.

As he picked up the trash, he came across the now-rumpled *Numismatist Weekly*. He saw a headline circled with bright red marker and looked at it more closely. The article was titled, "Coin Hoard Found in Trunk."

His father didn't collect coins — why would he want to read about them? Timmy shrugged and put the newspaper back in the wastebasket.

Deciding to go for a walk, Timmy looked around until he found some spare keys and then left the apartment, taking his camcorder and backpack along with him.

He wandered around outside until he found a convenience store, where he bought a bottle of Pepsi and a package of frosted doughnuts. Then he carried them to a nearby park and sat down on a bench to eat, and to film everything around him.

He aimed his camcorder at the city skyline and started shooting it. When he got bored by that, he tilted the lens down and focused on a father who was pushing his young daughter on a swing about fifty feet away.

Timmy filmed them for a while, then lowered the camera, looking at them wistfully. If only *his* father was like that. He didn't expect Ray to be the All-American father; he just wished that he would make an *effort*.

He had almost no memories involving his father, and the few that he did have were lousy. He remembered being five years old, and playing football out in the yard in front of his house. Then the police cars pulled up.

The next thing he knew, his father was being led out of the house in handcuffs while neighbors gathered across the street, watching the scene and talking in shocked whispers. Timmy felt his mother's hands reaching out to pull him into the house, and the last thing he saw was his father glancing back at them with shame and guilt in his eyes, just before he was put in the back of the police car.

"Hey," a voice said. "Your parents around, sport?"

Timmy shook his head to clear away the memory and looked up at a whacked-out derelict, who was greedily eyeing the camcorder.

"Yeah," Timmy said, and nodded in the direction of the man pushing his giggling daughter on the swing. "That's my dad."

As the derelict turned to look at the man, who was now walking away from the swings with his daughter, Timmy grabbed his camcorder and backpack and ran away as fast as he could. He remembered that he had left his doughnuts and soda behind, but the derelict was already eating them, and he certainly wasn't about to go back over there.

If his father cared enough to spend time with him and not let him walk around the city alone — things like this wouldn't happen.

Now where was he going to go?

Chapter 6

The robbery was planned for that afternoon.

Bobbie spent the day in his apartment, getting ready. He laid out various burglar's tools on his kitchen table, deciding which ones he was going to take. A good thief needed *just* the right equipment. He sat there, drinking coffee and admiring the array of pliers, screwdrivers, wire cutters, and splicers. Whenever there was a sale at Radio Shack, he was always the first one in line.

Right in the middle of the table, he had put his 9mm Beretta. He looked at the gun, then nodded, and picked it up, ramming in a full clip.

He was going to be ready for *anything*.

Across town, Carl was also at home in his apartment, but he was spending his time worrying about what to wear. As far as he was concerned, the worst thing about going to prison had been the *outfits*.

He put on a pair of sparkling clean, white painter's overalls and admired himself in a full-length mirror. He was so brilliantly white that he looked like Mr. Clean. He smiled at his reflection and took out a handkerchief, buffing one of the brass buttons.

A good thief was a fashionable one.

Ray was over at the bakery, having a meeting with the owner, Mr. Wankmueller. Mr. Wankmueller was about seventy, and beginning to think about retiring. Ray was eager to take over the business and had put together some sketches to show his boss how he would expand the bakery.

"I thought I'd knock out that wall there," he said, showing Mr. Wankmueller the mock-up blueprint. "Then push through, and that's where I'd put the bagel operation."

Mr. Wankmueller raised bushy white eyebrows. "Bagels?"

Ray nodded confidently. "Mr. Wankmueller, if you sell to me, not only do I continue the fine tradition of Wankmueller cakes, cookies, and bread, but I *also* give the public the highest-quality Wankmueller bagel."

"Hmmm," Mr. Wankmueller said, and perused the sketches, mulling all of this over. "*If* I sell."

Ray sighed, running his hands back through his hair — his all-purpose gesture of frustration. "You've been talking about doing that every day for the last two years, sir. And I've got the financing already lined up."

Mr. Wankmueller looked up from the plans and smiled. He liked Ray; he always had. "You're a good baker, Ray. But — "

"Look, Mr. Wankmueller," Ray said quickly, taking one last shot. "I know I was a bum before you gave me a chance here.

But I *know* I can make this place go. And if you sell to me, sir, you're not only selling to a good baker, you're selling to a guy who's now and forever a respectable, hard-working, one hundred percent law-abiding citizen." He gave Mr. Wankmueller a big, trustworthy smile to emphasize that.

"Hmmm," Mr. Wankmueller said, and bent over the sketches again, studying the changes Ray had in mind.

A few hours later, Ray was busy being a somewhat less than one-hundred-percent law-abiding citizen. He sat in the passenger's seat of the getaway van, wearing paint-splattered overalls, even more tense than he usually was before pulling a job.

Carl, who drove the van, was dressed in his blindingly white and pristine Mr. Clean outfit.

Nervously, Ray pulled on a pair of work gloves. "Now I want this job going down smooth. Everything according to plan." He eyed Carl's overalls. "We're *supposed* to be painters, you know. You look like you're going on a space mission."

Carl smiled benignly and put on his right-turn blinker before changing lanes, driving exactly at the speed limit.

Ray took out two Mace-like cylinders from his blue Nike travel bag, showing them to Carl.

"Here," he said. "Cayenne pepper. Super-concentrated. So don't go spraying it on your taco, eh?"

Carl nodded.

They rode in silence for a minute, Ray going over everything in his mind one more time. He had planned this job right down to the last detail, but he still wondered whether they could pull it off. Then, suddenly, a very different thought jumped into his mind.

"You know my kid's in the ninety-fifth percentile?" he said.

Carl looked at him blankly, having no idea what that might mean.

"How about that?" Ray said, and smiled.

Timmy wandered up and down unfamiliar streets, his backpack feeling increasingly heavy. As he passed a bank parking lot, he saw a BMW pull in and park in a handicapped parking space. A business-man — who looked very able-bodied — got out and strode toward the bank entrance.

"Excuse me, sir," Timmy said.

The man stopped and turned, seeing Timmy pointing his camcorder at him.

"I'm with Eyewitness News," Timmy said authoritatively. "The space you parked in is for handicapped drivers only. So I think you'd better move your car."

The businessman looked him over and then shook his head in annoyance. "Buzz off, you little twerp," he said, and went into the bank.

Timmy didn't like being called "little," he didn't like being called a "twerp," and he *really* didn't like people who parked in handicapped spaces. He shut off his cam-corder and looked around the nearby street for inspiration.

Down the block, he saw a doughnut shop — with a police car parked out in front. Timmy grinned, and trotted down to find the police officer who belonged to the car.

He was going to *enjoy* upholding this law.

*   *   *

When the businessman came out of the bank, he saw — to his shock and dismay — that a cop was writing him a ticket. The cop was taking his time, leaning up against the hood of the car, a box of fresh doughnuts resting beside him. He had a chocolate-glazed sitting on his upraised leg, and every few words, he stopped writing and took a bite from the doughnut.

"Hey, what is this?" the businessman asked, sounding outraged.

The cop barely looked up. "Looks like a twenty-two five-oh-seven — illegal parking in a handicapped zone," he said in a deep, no-nonsense voice. "And a thirty-three twenty-six, disobedience to signs."

Timmy, munching away on one of the doughnuts, popped up from behind the car. "And the little tag on the license plate?" he said, pointing. "It says 1991."

The cop nodded, scribbling the information down. "That's an eight-oh-seven. Expired tags." He licked the end of his pencil, flipped a page in his book, and started writing out another ticket. He paused, glancing at the fuming businessman. "Oh. Hey. Want a doughnut?"

"What are you, nuts? No, I don't want a doughnut!" the businessman yelled.

The cop shrugged, finishing his chocolate-glazed and selecting a powdered jelly doughnut next. "They're good, though. Trust me. I'm a cop. It's my *job* to know doughnuts." He bit into the jelly doughnut, chewed a few times, swallowed, and then patted his mouth with a napkin. "Can I see your registration, sir?"

"This is ridiculous!" the businessman protested, checking his watch in exasperation. "I have a very important appointment."

The cop just looked at him.

"I don't have it on me, okay?" the businessman said, more pleasantly. "I think I — lost it."

The cop took that in, and then nodded solemnly, licking the end of his pencil. "No registration card — eight-oh-two." He scanned his ticket book, referring back to the infractions he had already written down. "Well, let's see what we got here. . . . A twenty-two five-oh-seven, a thirty-three twenty-six, an eight-oh-seven, and an eight-oh-two." He paused. "Know what that adds up to?"

Timmy thought for a second. "Twenty-seven thousand, four hundred and forty-two?"he guessed.

"*Exactly,*" the cop said. He tore off the tickets and handed them to the business-man with a smile. "Thank God for con-cerned citizens, right, sir?"

The businessman was speechless.

Timmy also smiled at the open-mouthed businessman. "Well — better buzz," he said, helped himself to another doughnut for the road, and strolled away.

Chalk up another one for law and order.

At the office building housing the Cer-tified Coin Grading Service, it was almost quitting time. Workmen on the second floor were methodically throwing wallboard ma-terial down the chute to the Dumpster in the alley, when one of them looked at his watch and indicated to the others that it was time to call it a day. They nodded and immediately stopped what they were doing, took off their hard hats, and headed for the time clock to punch out.

Down in the street, Bobbie, who was wearing his own hard hat and carrying a toolbox, stopped in front of the building. He looked up to see the van carrying Ray and Carl stop and park farther down the alley. He and Ray made eye contact, both nodded, and Bobbie headed into the building to put the first part of the plan into action.

He crossed the office building lobby to the two elevators as workmen, who were on their way home, came down the stairs from the second floor. Bobbie pressed the "Up" button and the left elevator doors opened. He entered, glanced around, and then taped a yellow "OUT OF ORDER" banner across the doorway.

Once he had finished, he pressed the "Hold" button on the elevator panel, and then bent down to open his toolbox. The 9mm Beretta was in among the various tools. He moved it aside, selected a screwdriver, and started unscrewing the panel to get at the wiring inside.

Outside, Ray waited for the last of the workmen to exit the building. He glanced at Carl with a trace of uncertainty in his eyes.

"We can do it, Ray," Carl said, eating a candy bar in two bites. "No sweat."

Ray nodded, needing this last jolt of confidence. Then he took a deep breath and got out of the van. He and Carl walked casually into the building, carrying paint cans, brushes, rollers, and the blue Nike bag.

Still inside the elevator, Bobbie cut two wires, a red one and a blue one. Then, using alligator clips, he rewired them to each other, completely changing the original circuitry. He worked swiftly, but cautiously, knowing that even the slightest mistake would ruin everything. He had *no* interest in going back to jail.

"We're in," Ray's voice said, filtered through static as it came over the Toys "R" Us walkie-talkie in Bobbie's shirt pocket.

Bobbie pressed the "Talk" button to answer. "Detour's wired," he said.

"Roger," Ray responded, his voice crackling through the receiver. He pulled in another deep breath. "Let's do it."

Chapter 7

Timmy had finally gotten tired of walking aimlessly around the city by himself and gone back to Ray's apartment. There, he sprawled on the couch and watched an old James Bond movie on television.

"Bond. James Bond," he said, and imitated Bond's debonair movements as he shook his Pepsi can. "Shaken, not stirred."

He popped open the can, and the soda promptly sprayed all over his face.

Not so debonair, after all.

He wiped some of the soda off with a corner of the army blanket and settled back to watch the rest of the movie. It was pretty good, but he couldn't help wondering where his father was, and what he might be doing.

Timmy just hoped that whatever it was, it was legal.

In the office building, Ray was now on the second floor. He looked out a window at the driveway leading to the underground parking level, and saw an armored car drive down it. Instantly, he clicked on his Toys "R" Us walkie-talkie.

"Rent-a-cop has arrived," he said, and clicked off.

Hearing that, Bobbie removed the "OUT OF ORDER" banner from the left elevator, got into the right elevator, and taped the banner across it, instead. Once again, he pressed the "Hold" button and got ready to do his rewiring.

Just then, he heard footsteps and voices approaching. When he grabbed his gun from his tool chest, it slipped from his grasp and clattered to the elevator floor, in full view. But, luckily, the people — workmen, mostly — walked by without seeming to notice it, or *him*. Bobbie snatched up his gun and put it away, heaving a sigh of relief.

So far, their luck was holding.

Down in the parking level, the armored car pulled up next to the elevator bank. Two guards climbed out, leaving the driver inside. They pressed the "Up" button, and the left elevator — the one Bobby had already rewired — opened.

The two men got inside and rode up to the sixth floor. They exited the elevator and crossed the foyer to a set of heavy glass doors marked CERTIFIED COIN GRADING SERVICE. A company guard at the front desk activated the door buzzer, letting them in.

Inside the coin vault, a company official was just finishing loading the slabbed coins into a metal carrying case. He double-checked the inventory one last time, and then closed and locked the case. He nodded at the company guards with him, and they all went out to the receiving area to complete the transfer.

The official gave the coins to the two guards from the armored car, and they left the Grading Service, returning to the elevators. The guard who wasn't holding the case pressed the call button, and the left elevator opened.

They stepped aboard without a second thought and pressed the button for the Parking level.

Waiting in the first floor lobby, Bobbie saw on the lighted floor indicator that the elevator was coming down.

"Nonstop to you," he said into his walkie-talkie. Then, his job done, he picked up his toolbox and left the building. All he could do now was wait for the others to meet him in the van.

The elevator opened on the second floor, revealing Ray, who was wearing a surgical mask and goggles to hide his face, while he pretended to paint a door marked "STAIRWAY" on the opposite wall.

The first guard, who wasn't holding the coins, pressed the "Parking" button, but the elevator didn't move.

"Let's walk down," his partner suggested,

the coin case gripped in his right hand.

The first guard nodded cautiously, but sensing that something was amiss, he unsnapped the safety strap on his holster and put his hand on the gun butt. Then, he nodded "okay" to the second guard.

As they got off the elevator — before they knew what was happening or saw who was doing it — Carl rushed in from the side and sprayed them in the face with cayenne pepper. Instantly incapacitated, the two guards went down, choking and coughing, rubbing frantically at the tears streaming from their eyes.

Carl and Ray grabbed their guns, dropping them in a nearby bucket of paint. All they needed was another couple of minutes, and the coins would be theirs.

Down on the parking level, the driver of the armored car was wondering why the guards were taking so long. He looked at his watch, and then flicked on his company-issue walkie-talkie.

"Charlie, what's taking you guys so long?" he asked.

Upstairs, Ray and Carl had pulled the choking guards into an empty office, tied them up, and gagged them. While Ray was putting blindfolds over their eyes, Carl cut open the coin case with a power tool they had brought along.

The driver's voice came over the walkie-talkies on the guards' belts, and one of the guards tried to mumble a response through his gag.

"Charlie?" the driver said again.

Thinking fast, Ray grabbed the nearest walkie-talkie, signalling for Carl to hurry up and transfer the coins into the Nike travel bag before he responded to the question.

"You mind?" Ray said, purposely muffling his voice and making himself sound aggrieved. "I had to make a pit stop."

"Where's Mel?" the driver asked.

Ray tried to think of a good answer but couldn't come up with one quickly enough. "He's uh, he's in here, too."

"You can't *both* go in there at the same time," the driver said. "That's against regulations!" Knowing that both guards were

62

well aware of that, he started to get very suspicious. "State your status!"

Ray looked at Carl, who shrugged.

"State your status!" the driver ordered over the walkie-talkie.

Ray mouthed the word "Run!" at Carl, dropped the walkie-talkie, and they both took off with the blue Nike bag.

"Holy moly!" the driver said down in his truck. He fumbled for the microphone on the dashboard. "Possible two-eleven in progress! All units respond! Repeat, Two-eleven in progress!"

Chapter 8

Ray and Carl ran down the hallway and into the office with the construction chute. Ray jumped inside the chute and slid down into the Dumpster. Carl jumped in right after him but the back of his overalls got caught on a protruding edge, and he hung there, dangling helplessly at the top of the chute.

Ray leaped out of the Dumpster just as Bobbie came driving up in the van and screeched to a stop next to it.

In the distance, they could hear police sirens.

"Come on! Come on!" Ray yelled over

his shoulder, not sure what was taking Carl so long.

"I'm stuck, Ray!" Carl yelled back.

The police sirens came closer and closer as Carl frantically tried to free himself. Finally, the cloth ripped loose, and he slid down the chute, landing in a pile of dust. He scrambled up and out of the Dumpster. Ray used both hands to drag him into the van as Bobbie pressed the accelerator to the floor.

"No!" Ray said. "Slow, *slow*. Take it easy."

Bobbie eased up on the gas, and they drove sedately away from the scene of the crime as two police cars whipped past them on their way to the robbery.

They all breathed more easily and broke into wide smiles, realizing that they had gotten away. Carl let out a whoop, and gave Ray a high-five. Bobbie turned to high-five Carl, but didn't see a police car, its sirens and lights going, as it made an unexpected left turn right in front of them. Bobbie looked forward and jammed on the brakes just in time, missing a fatal collision by inches.

The police car continued on toward the robbery, and Bobbie continued driving down the street *away* from it. For a minute they all held their breaths, and then slowly let them out.

"How about we don't celebrate just yet," Ray said, his voice shaking.

Bobbie and Carl nodded, still too scared to speak.

They drove, following every single traffic law that existed, until they were *sure* that they had gotten away cleanly. Bobbie stopped the van on a deserted side street, and they all jumped out, playfully tossing the bag of coins around as if it were a medicine ball.

Ray and Carl peeled off their painter's coveralls in striptease fashion, and then Bobbie joined them as they danced around with unbridled happiness.

This moment of triumph was the high point of their entire lives.

Back at the apartment, Timmy was still lying on the couch, watching television. The movie had ended, and now he was switching from sitcom to sitcom, each one more familiar than the last.

It was dark out, and his father should have already gotten home from work — but he hadn't. Didn't he even care if Timmy got dinner or not? Didn't he care about *anything*?

Tired of the rerun he was watching, Timmy changed the channel, getting the local news. He was going to hit the channel selector again but decided to listen for a minute or two.

A newscaster was standing in front of a brick office building downtown, talking about a robbery that had apparently occurred that afternoon.

". . .where this afternoon, two armed guards were robbed of one and a half million dollars in rare coins," the reporter was saying.

Timmy watched, something clicking inside his mind.

The reporter was now gesturing toward the top floor of the building. "The guards had just picked up the coins here from the Certified Coin Grading Service, when two men overpowered them on the second floor, tied them up, and made off with the fortune in coins."

Timmy jumped off the couch and ran into his father's bedroom, retrieving the copy of the *Numismatist Weekly* from the wastepaper basket. Quickly, he skimmed the "Coin Hoard Found in Trunk" article, until he came to the words, "valued at $1.5 million."

"One-point-five million," Timmy said aloud, and let the paper fall from his hands, feeling stunned.

There was no doubt in his mind who had pulled that robbery.

Ray and his friends drove the van to where they had parked Ray's car earlier, and then left the van behind. With luck, it would never be traced to them. Then they all piled into Ray's car, and he drove to a phone booth so that he could call their fence and confirm that they had the coins and were ready to make a deal. As he made the call, Carl and Bobbie stood nearby to listen in.

"No, no, *no*," Ray said impatiently. "The

deal is C.O.D." He listened for a minute. "Okay, how much time do you need?" He listened again, shaking his head. "This is *not* the way we agreed to — okay, okay, if that's what you need, fine. See you then." He frowned and hung up the phone.

"Well?" Carl asked.

"Change of plans," Ray said.

Bobbie's eyes narrowed. "What do you mean, change of plans?"

Ray shrugged matter-of-factly. "Dobbs needs more time to raise the cash. He'll have it Sunday."

"Sunday? That's six days!" Bobbie protested. "What do we do with the coins until then?"

"Trust me," Ray said, and got back into the car.

Bobbie looked skeptical, but opened the passenger's side door, while Carl climbed amiably into the back.

"Everything's under control," Ray promised, and turned on the ignition.

When the car pulled up in front of Ray's apartment building, Timmy heard it and raced to the window with his camcorder.

He planned to get *every bit* of this on tape.

His father stepped out of the car, carrying the Nike bag full of coins. Carl and Bobbie followed him. They were all standing right underneath a street lamp, and Timmy used the zoom lens to film their faces, which were fully visible and recognizable under the light.

The tape was going to make *great* evidence.

Chapter 9

"Come on," Ray said. "This won't take long."

He led them inside and up the stairs, motioning for them to be very quiet. After they passed the apartment door, Timmy peeked out and watched them as they headed for a stairwell door that led up to the roof.

"Up here," Ray said, and opened the door.

Timmy waited for them to clear out of the hall, and then crept out after them.

Once they were on the roof, Ray used a screwdriver to pry loose bricks from a barbecue pit that was built onto the side of a storage shed.

"How come we're hiding it at *your* place?" Bobbie wanted to know.

"Because no one's going to find it here," Ray said, lifting the bricks out and placing them to one side. "Nobody ever comes up here."

"Yeah, right," Bobbie said cynically. "Nobody comes up here? You don't think *you'll* be tempted to come up and visit when we're not around? Huh?" He looked over at Carl, appealing for support.

Carl didn't say anything, as always, thinking it through first.

"I want my share *now*, Ray," Bobbie said. "We split here and now."

Ray sighed. "We can't split now. Every one of these coins is worth a different amount. When we get the money, *that's* when we split."

"Sounds right to me," Carl said slowly.

Bobbie looked from one of them to the other, realizing that he was outnumbered. He was about to complain when he heard a creak from the stairwell door.

"Hey!" he said. "Somebody's there."

Ray rolled his eyes at Carl, believing that Bobbie had just conjured up yet another boogeyman.

In the meantime, Timmy shrank away from the door, afraid that he had been seen.

Bobbie strode across the roof and jerked the door open, revealing . . . no one. He crept down the steps and looked out into the hallway, but there was nobody there. He lit a cigarette, the match light illuminating Timmy, who was crouched behind some boxes under the steps. But Bobbie didn't see him and just shook out the match and went back up to the roof.

Ray was replacing the last brick over the hole hiding the Nike bag when Bobbie reappeared.

"What'ja find there, Bob?" he asked. "Mike Wallace and the Sixty Minutes crew?"

Carl chuckled appreciatively; Bobbie scowled.

"There." Ray stood up, dusting off his hands. "Safe as Fort Knox. Come on, beers are on me."

"Okay," Bobbie said grudgingly. "But until we move that — I'm watching you."

Ray nodded, humoring him, and they went downstairs past his apartment.

"I'd better check on my kid," he said.

"Yeah, sure, the doting father," Bobbie said, folding his arms across his chest. "We'll wait."

Ray shrugged and unlocked the door. Seeing the television on and Timmy asleep on the couch, he walked over and looked down at his son — a little cherub in beatific repose. Relieved that everything seemed to be under control, Ray went back out to the hall.

As the door closed, Timmy's eyes popped open, gleaming with anticipated revenge.

He was not going to let his father get away with this.

Ray drove them all to a nearby bar, a working-class watering hole where they went regularly. Bobbie was still sulking, so he sat up at the bar by himself, while Ray and Carl sat together in a booth.

"You know what I'm going to do, Ray?" Carl asked. "Take a cruise. First-class, around the world. They got good food on those boats, Ray."

Ray nodded, drinking some of his beer. "Yeah, and you have to dress for dinner. You'll like that."

Carl looked very pleased as he reached down to straighten his tie. "And maybe I'll meet a nice little lady who wants to make me her reform project."

Ray laughed, and they clinked their beer bottles in a toast.

In the meantime, Bobbie sat up at the bar, scheming. He didn't trust anyone — including his two best friends. As long as the coins were out of his hands, he wasn't going to relax for a second. No one was going to pull the wool over *his* eyes.

Sitting in the booth, Ray looked into his beer, deep in thought.

"Must feel good, huh, Ray?" Carl said. "Maybe getting that bakery, being your own boss."

That was what Ray had always wanted — and it was almost in his grasp. His dream was so close he could practically taste it.

"I knew if I could get one big score, I could turn the corner," he said softly. "And this is it, Carl, this is my big chance. For the first time in my life, I've got a future."

Carl nodded. "I hear ya, man. Everyone needs something solid to hang on to, you know? Especially people like us, because if we don't have that, we'll be back in the joint. And next time, it'll be for good."

Ray frowned, knowing that that was true.

"But that's not going to happen," Carl said, his face brightening, "because you had this thing figured, Ray. You didn't miss a trick."

Ray gave a modest shrug. "It's all in the planning, Carl. See, you don't just go squirting frosting on a cake. You have to think it through."

Carl nodded, determined to follow this entire conversation without getting confused.

"You create a design, you draw it up, you make it beautiful," Ray said, gesturing expansively. "You mix up frosting of the perfect taste and consistency, the perfect color. . . ."

"Yeah," Carl agreed. "Yeah, I hear ya, man."

"And if you do all that," Ray said, "then

you know — you *know* that when the job is finished, it's going to come out exactly the way you wanted it."

Carl grinned broadly. "And we did it, Ray. Nobody can take that away from us."

They clinked their bottles together again and drank another toast.

After retrieving the Nike travel bag from its bricked hiding place, Timmy carried it out of the apartment building. When he got to the street, he stopped and looked both ways.

It was time to put his plan into action.

He moved down the sidewalk and stopped at a mailbox. He pulled a lumpy manila envelope from his jacket and put it in the mail slot. Then he set off down the sidewalk at a brisk, purposeful pace, carrying the Nike bag.

There was a cable car waiting just up ahead, and he hopped onto it and sat down as the car started its climb up the hill and into the night.

Chapter 10

Ray and Carl were still sitting in their booth when Carl happened to glance at the bar and saw that Bobbie wasn't there anymore.

"Hey, where's Bobbie?" he asked.

Ray shook himself from his thoughts and saw that Bobbie was gone.

"Come on," he said, hurrying toward the men's room, with the dreadful feeling that they were going to be too late.

When he opened the door, he saw Bobbie standing on top of the toilet, trying to climb out the small bathroom window.

"Going somewhere, Bob?" he asked.

Startled, Bobbie slipped off the toilet seat, his foot landing inside the toilet. His hand grabbed the flush handle and he flushed water onto his shoe and pants leg.

"I was going for my share of the coins, okay?!" he said defensively. "That's all I want, *my* share."

Ray checked to make sure that the room was empty. "Bob, how many times do I have to tell you — "

"We can split 'em three ways," Bobbie interrupted. "And then when Dobbs comes, we bring our stashes together, and we split the cash even." He clenched his fist. "Do it my way, or you're going to have to worry every time I'm out of your sight, Ray. That clear?" Then he walked out of the men's room, his shoe making a squishing sound with each step.

Ray sighed, catching sight of his worried expression in the cracked mirror. His elaborate plan, so perfectly devised, was starting to unravel.

He would have been even more worried if he had known that there was a wino sitting outside, under the open window, who had heard every word of their conversation.

Across town, the San Francisco police had cordoned off a murder scene and had begun to proceed with the crime scene investigation. Uniformed and plainsclothes officers milled about, keeping onlookers away from the dead body, which lay on the sidewalk, covered by a tarp.

Lieutenant Romayko, a squat, overweight man, crouched next to the corpse, peering under the bloodstained tarp while calmly eating a banana. MacReady, a female detective in her forties, stood off to the side, watching and making an occasional note.

Behind them, an unmarked police car pulled up, jerking to a stop. Lieutenant Romayko looked over his shoulder to see who it was and winced.

Gung-ho rookie detective Theresa Walsh jumped out of the driver's side of the car. A slim young woman in her late twenties, she was all cop — and dressed, spoke, and *lived* that way.

Alex Ceranski, her partner, took his time getting out from the passenger's side, although he and Theresa were obviously in the middle of an argument.

"Did too," Alex said.

"I did *not*," Theresa insisted.

Alex let out an annoyed breath. "Walsh, you came *this* close to hitting the cable car. I mean, you shot your *last* partner in the foot. You trying to get rid of me with a heart attack?"

Theresa flushed. "How many times do you have to bring that up? I told you — my gun discharged; it was an accident. And if you want to drive from now on, here" — she tossed him the car keys — "be my guest."

As she turned to walk to the crime scene, she came face to face with a stern Lieutenant Romayko, MacReady backing him up, her expression concerned.

"Oh, uh — Lieutenant," Theresa said, standing up straighter. "I mean — sir. We might have a lead on that coin robbery."

Lieutenant Romayko took a small bite of his banana, doing his best to speak in a measured voice. "Is that so, Walsh," he said without much interest. "Tell me, did you happen to notice this is a crime scene?"

"Well — " Theresa stopped and looked around at all of the activity. "Yes, sir. Sure did, sir."

Lieutenant Romayko nodded and turned to his partner. "MacReady, what's the most important thing at a crime scene?" he asked.

"Evidence," MacReady said.

"Evidence," Lieutenant Romayko agreed. "Exactly. And you know what you just did, Walsh?" He pointed with what was left of his banana. "You *ran over* evidence."

Theresa looked down at the street and grimaced. In the track of her front tire, lying in a carefully drawn chalk circle, was a shell casing from the murder, now completely crushed.

Lieutenant Romayko picked it up, holding it gently by the edges. "Now, how are we going to match this shell casing to the murder weapon?"

"Oh," Theresa said, her face red with humiliation. "Gee, I — I'm very sorry, sir."

Lieutenant Romayko just let his eyes bore into her, while Detective MacReady gave her a sympathetic shrug. Alex sighed and eyed the heavens above.

"Luckily, we found other casings," Lieutenant Romayko said, relenting slightly. "But for somebody already on probation, I'd think you'd be a little more careful, Walsh." He paused. "Ceranski, I want you to drive from now on."

Alex dangled the keys from his right hand. "That's already been arranged, Lieutenant."

"Good. And Walsh — " Lieutenant Romayko dropped his banana peel in her hand. "Take care of this." He walked off, leaving her holding the peel.

Alex tried to lighten the atmosphere with a joke. "Hey, at least you didn't run over the body."

Theresa shot him a "drop dead" look, and tossed the banana peel into the nearest trash can.

At Bobbie's insistence, he and Ray and Carl left the bar and went back to the hiding place on the roof to divide up the coins.

"Okay," Ray said, as they walked out onto the roof. "Each one of us reaches into the bag and grabs a coin. We do this until they're all gone. And I don't want anyone complaining about what coin they get, because it's all by chance — "

They stopped, seeing that the bricks had been pulled away from the hiding place. After everyone exchanged shocked looks, Ray dove for the hole, groping around inside for the bag.

"It's . . . gone," he said, barely able to believe it.

"Gone?" Bobbie yelled. "*Gone?*" Crazed with fury, he shoved Ray aside and began pulling away more bricks, thrusting his entire torso into the empty hole.

That was when Timmy stepped out onto the roof from the stairwell door.

"Excuse me, guys," he said, pleasantly.

They all whirled around to stare at him.

Timmy smiled. "I think it's time for us to have a little talk," he said.

They ended up downstairs in Ray's kitchen, where Timmy prolonged the agony by fixing himself a peanut-butter sandwich, pouring a tall glass of milk, and sitting down to eat.

"After I raided your hiding place," he said conversationally, "I spread the coins here on the table and videotaped them with my camera." He touched his camcorder fondly. "I also got some good shots of you coming into the building, so I'm sure the cops will have *no* trouble identifying you."

"Oh, you did, did you?" Bobbie said, standing up so abruptly that his chair shot out from underneath him. "What are you trying to pull, you little weasel!"

Ray held up a silencing hand before the situation could deteriorate even more. "*Bob*," he said, and then looked calmly at Timmy. "Go on, Tim."

Timmy shrugged, taking another bite of his sandwich. "The videotape is on its way to a friend of mine, along with a letter that tells the whole story."

Ray smiled. "Okay, Tim," he said, and laughed good-naturedly. "You got us. Right, guys? Let's admit it, he's got us."

Taking the cue, Carl chimed in with a cheery laugh, while Bobbie just glared malevolently.

"So," Ray said, very calm. "The coins, Tim. *Where* are the coins?"

Timmy finished his milk. "Wouldn't *you* like to know."

"That cuts it!" Bobbie said. "When I sassed my old man, he took his belt to me — the *same thing* I'm going to do to you!" He started removing his belt, but in his fit of anger, he tried to pull the metal part through the belt loops and got it all jammed up.

Ray grabbed both of his arms to keep him still. "Just hold on, Bob."

"Let me go, Ray!" Bobbie said, trying to yank free. "*I'll* get the little punk to talk!"

Timmy scrambled around Ray's back, instinctively taking refuge behind the safety of his father.

"I said, hold on!" Ray yelled, doing his best to keep them apart. "Nobody's going to hurt anyone here!"

"That's right!" Timmy said, sticking his head out from behind Ray's back. "Because if *anything* happens to me — if I don't call my friend every night and give him a *new* password, he's taking that video straight to the cops. And you'll *all* go to prison for a long, long time!"

The men exchanged looks, absorbing this threat. It was clear that Timmy took after his father — he had thought of everything.

They were going to have to play by *his* rules.

Chapter 11

Bobbie was the first one to react to this turn of events and, looking for something — anything — to smash, he grabbed Ray's toaster oven and threw it against the wall as hard as he could.

"Hey," Ray protested, looking down at the wreckage. "You broke my toaster oven. Why'd you do that?"

"Because I'm upset!" Bobbie shouted. "And when I get upset, I gotta *vent!*"

Ray grabbed him by the lapels, drawing one fist back as Bobbie recoiled.

"*You* are buying me a new toaster oven," Ray said, holding his fist up threateningly.

"Okay, Ray, all right!" Bobbie promised. "I didn't know it was a family heirloom."

After giving him a long hard look, Ray let him go. Then he returned his attention to Timmy.

"Okay, Tim," he said, sounding very reasonable. "I haven't exactly been the model father. You're angry, I understand. But I still *am* your father. And I know you'd never rat on your own flesh and blood."

"Just try me," Timmy said, deadly serious.

The men exchanged looks. Clearly, this kid meant business.

"I'm going to find the coins," Bobbie said, and started rifling through the kitchen cabinets, tossing out pots and pans. In a frenzy, he moved on to the living room, pulling cushions from the couch and digging through a wastebasket in growing desperation.

Carl worked at a more leisurely pace, checking the hall closet and the bathroom. Catching a glimpse of himself in the medicine cabinet mirror, he took a moment to smooth his hair and practice his smile — and was very pleased by the results.

Ray searched through the laundry room in the basement and in the Dumpster behind the building. When he didn't find anything, he went back up to his bedroom to search it again.

Timmy watched as his father sprawled on the floor, looking under the bed, finding nothing but clumps of dust.

"Right, Dad," he said, leaning in the doorway. "Like I'd be dumb enough to hide it here. You're not even warm."

After searching for a couple of hours without success, the men gave up and sat down in the kitchen to discuss further strategy, as Timmy watched television on the living room couch.

"He could have rented a locker somewhere," Ray said in a low voice. "Like at one of those storage places."

Bobbie nodded. "Or the airport, or the bus station. It could be a *million* places." Then he thought of something. "What if he didn't send anything to his friend? What if he's bluffing? You know, he could be bluffing."

They all swiveled their heads to look at Timmy, who smiled confidently at them.

"He's not bluffing," Ray said grimly, aware that his future as a bakery owner was slipping away. "I think I'm going to kill him."

"Now you're talking — we *make* him tell us." Bobbie stood up with his fists clenched, ready for violence. "Come on, let's — "

Ray pulled him back. "Look, if anybody's going to kill him, *I'll* kill him. You understand?"

Bobbie nodded sheepishly.

Ray went over to the living room couch, making a supreme effort not to lose his temper.

"Okay, Tim, you've had your fun," he said. "But now I need to know. What do you want?"

"He wants in on the deal, that's what," Bobbie said sulkily. "But he's not getting any of my share. He's your kid — you split with him."

Timmy shook his head. "I don't want any money. I think stealing is wrong."

"You think stealing is wrong," Bobbie said, sneering. "Then why did you *steal* the coins from us?!"

Ray sent him another warning glance.

He might not be the best parent in the world, but if anyone was going to yell at his kid, it was going to be *him*.

"You've got this all wrong, Tim," he said. "Do you know who those coins belong to?"

Timmy shrugged. "Well, me right now."

Ray shook his head, sitting on the couch next to him. "They don't belong to any-body," he said. "They used to belong to an old lady, but she died, and the govern-ment — the state — confiscated them. They *stole* them, Tim."

Timmy didn't buy *that* concept for a minute.

"Anyway," Ray went on. "Now they're going to sell them, and you know where that money goes? To buy limousines for fat-cat politicians, that's where. Now, what am *I* going to do with the money?"

Timmy shrugged, not sure if he even cared.

"I'm buying the bakery where I work, Tim," Ray said, sounding proud. "I'm going to expand and hire more people. Those peo-ple will pay taxes, and eventually, the gov-ernment gets its money back. And your *dad's* got a respectable business, he's through with crime, he's *straight*."

Was his father expecting that argument to hit home? "So," Timmy spoke slowly, "you're saying you want to go straight — and that to do that you have to steal."

Ray was going to agree, but the logic was a little hard to justify.

"I'm eleven, and that seems dumb even to me," Timmy said.

Bobbie growled something unintelligible, and then shook his fist. "I say we hang him off the roof by his ankles. Let's vote!"

At the moment Ray couldn't help thinking that the idea had a certain appeal.

"Just tell me what you *want*," he said to Timmy, inches from exploding.

Timmy considered that for a long minute. "Ever since I got here, you've ignored me."

"I was planning a robbery, son," Ray said, and then finally lost his temper. "What'd you *expect* me to do — take you *camping*?"

That was the exact sort of thing Timmy had expected. He pulled from his pocket the itinerary he had written and unfolded it. "You want to know what I want?" he asked. "I want *this*."

Ray snatched the paper from his hand, and scanned the list. "What is this? The aquarium, The Giants game, the museum . . ." He frowned at Timmy. "What, you want to go to all of these places?"

"I want *you* to take me," Timmy said. "I want you to pretend you like having me around for the week. And, if you do real good, Dad, I'll tell you where the coins are." He stood up with a big yawn. "Well, I'm turning in. I'll be sleeping in your bed. *You* take the couch." He walked down the hall and disappeared into his father's bedroom, shutting the door.

Ray, Bobbie, and Carl stood there, looking at each other.

"I can't believe this," Bobbie said finally. "We're being blackmailed by an *eleven-year-old*."

Chapter 12

Over at the precinct house, Theresa and Alex had brought in their informant on the coin robbery to tell his story. After taping the interrogation, they brought the videotape into Lieutentant Romayko's office to show it to him.

On the tape, the wino was sitting hunched at a table in a small windowless room, puffing on a cigarette, and talking to Detective Zinn, another officer.

"So," Zinn said, "you were out in the alley, and you heard two men arguing in the rest room about splitting their share of the coins."

The wino nodded. "Yep."

"And you're sure their names were Bob and Ray," Zinn said.

"Yep, Bob and Ray," the wino agreed. "You know, like those guys used to be on the radio? Whatever happened to them? They were funny — "

Zinn waved his hand, trying to bring him back to the subject. "And you think their fence was someone named Dobbs?"

"Yep." The wino leaned across the table. "Now what about my money? You said I get fifty bucks for — "

At that, Lieutenant Romayko abruptly clicked off the television, shaking his head with disgust.

Alex frowned at Theresa. "*This* is our informant? Some guy from Wino's "R" Us?"

"That true, Walsh?" Lieutenant Romayko asked, looking up from the array of vitamins and pills on his desk as he methodically took one pill from each bottle and swallowed it with slugs of cold coffee. "This is your 'lead'?"

"Well — " Theresa hesitated. "Sir, the Brinks guards couldn't give us a description. They got sprayed with — "

Alex stood up. "Lieutenant, we'll come back when we have something solid to present."

"Wait, I *do* have something," Theresa said. "I think."

Alex sagged back down into his chair, covering his face with his hands.

"Can we hear it before my arteries harden?" Lieutenant Romayko asked.

"Yes, sir." This was her big chance to prove herself, and Theresa grabbed the floor. "Based on what the wino said, I cross-checked the names of local perps — er, perpetrators — who've worked together in the past. I came up with these two. Bobbie Drace and Ray Gleason." She handed a folder each to Alex and Lieutenant Romayko.

They opened the folders, revealing Bobbie's and Ray's mug shots and rap sheets.

"Grand theft, mail fraud . . ." Lieutenant Romayko read aloud.

"Penny-ante stuff," Alex said, dismissing the whole thing. "Come on, some juicer thinks he hears a couple of names, and — "

Pressing on, Theresa produced a computer printout. "I also did some checking through NCIC," she said, referring to a national data base that tracked criminal activity. "There've been four major coin robberies in the last two years. Each time, an auction house or coin grading company was hit."

"You're saying *these* clowns are behind all these jobs?" Alex asked dubiously.

Theresa shook her head. "No, but what if 'Dobbs' is? He has to be a specialist to move this stuff, right? Maybe he sets it all up and finds local talent to do the job. If these *are* the guys, then they're waiting for him, sir. This could be our break to solve *all* of these cases."

Lieutenant Romayko popped a vitamin, mulling this possibility over.

"Yeah. Right." Alex stood up. "Excuse me while I go solve the Kennedy assassination."

To her credit, Theresa let that pass. "All I'm saying is, if we pick up Gleason and Drace now, we'll scare off Dobbs. *But* if we put them on twenty-four-hour surveillance, and wait for Dobbs to show — we can nail them *all*."

Lieutenant Romayko didn't answer, as

he struggled with one of his vitamin bottles. "Darned safety caps," he said, and tossed the bottle to Alex, who opened it and handed it back. He gulped down a pill and looked at Theresa. "Okay, I'll give you a few days. But you better come up with something quick."

Alex scowled, upset that the Lieutenant was going along with this.

"You look like you've got food poisoning or something Ceranski," Lieutenant Romayko said. "You got something to add?"

Alex looked grim. "No, sir. The *rookie's* got it all figured out. I'm just the driver." He scowled at Theresa and left the room.

Theresa stood up more slowly, her enthusiasm somewhat crushed.

"Walsh," Lieutenant Romayko said after her. "The fact that I was good friends with your father — it won't cut you any ice. Your probation report is coming up, so don't blow this."

"I won't, sir," Theresa said, looking very determined. She watched as Lieutenant Romayko shook another vitamin into his hand. "Uh — you already took the bee pollen, sir."

He looked down at his hand in some confusion, trying to remember exactly *what* he had taken. Without question, the price of good health was eternal vigilance.

The next morning, Ray telephoned the bakery first thing, while Bobbie and Carl stood glumly by the front door, waiting to go. Timmy bounced around the living room, full of pep, wearing his backpack.

"Mr. Wankmueller, you know those vacation days I've been saving up?" Ray said into the phone. "Well, I kind of have this family emergency, and I need to take a few days off." He listened to his boss's response. "Great, thanks for understanding, Mr. Wankmueller. I'll make it up to you."

"Come on, the day's a-wasting!" Timmy shouted from the hall.

Ray, Bobbie, and Carl followed him out of the building, their dark moods contrasting with his bright one.

"I *hate* this," Bobbie growled.

Ray shrugged. "You don't have to come along, you know."

"Oh, no?" Bobbie asked. "Listen, 'Dad,' if he tells you where the coins are, *I'm* going to be there to hear it."

"Me, too," Carl said.

Ray shrugged, walking toward his car. "Your call, guys."

Across the street, Theresa and Alex were watching from inside an unmarked police car.

"What's with the kid?" Alex asked.

Using a telephoto lens, Theresa snapped off a few photos of Timmy and the men. Then she lowered the camera, studying Timmy, wondering what his connection was.

"I don't know," she said thoughtfully, and looked troubled.

Timmy opened the car door, making a face when he saw the mess on the seat and floor — soda cans, candy wrappers, and old fast-food bags strewn all over the place.

"Maid's day off, Dad?" he asked.

Ray swept the junk from the seat and onto the floor so Timmy could sit down. In the meantime, Carl and Bobbie got in the back.

Timmy turned to face them. "Okay, here are the rules. If you're coming along, you have to join in *all* the activities. Okay?"

"Sure, kid," Bobbie sneered. "We got it."

"Good." Timmy faced the front, and fastened his seat belt. "Seat belts."

Since they weren't exactly the kind of people who used seat belts, they just looked at him.

"It's the law," Timmy said, *"isn't* it?"

Bobbie nudged Carl with his elbow. "We do a boost worth a million five, but we have to worry about the seat-belt law."

"It's one of my rules," Timmy said.

Reluctantly, the three men fastened their seat belts.

"And could you put that out, please?" Timmy asked, indicating Bobbie's cigarette. "The smoke bothers me."

"I don't care if the smoke *poisons* you," Bobbie said.

Ray turned around. *"Bob.* Douse it."

Fuming, Bobbie jammed the cigarette into the ashtray.

"We can go now," Timmy said cheerfully.

Ray started the car and pulled out into the street.

Behind them, staying well back, Theresa and Alex followed in the unmarked police car.

Chapter 13

Theresa and Alex followed Ray's car to the aquarium.

"Aquarium?" Theresa said, confused. "What're they doing *here*?"

"Could be robbing the place," Alex said dryly, as he parked the car. "Any second now, they'll come running out with a porpoise under each arm."

"Or they could be meeting their contact," Theresa mused. "I'm going in." She put on a scarf and sunglasses, which, coupled with her conservative business suit, made her look rather ridiculous.

"What is that you're doing?" Alex asked.

She just looked at him.

"Oh, a *disguise*," he said. "*Very* effective."

She got out of the car without answering him, walking with utter dignity.

"They won't spot her," Alex said, and shook his head. "Oh, *no*. Not a chance."

Timmy and the guys entered the aquarium after Ray paid for everyone's admission. The lighting was dark and soothing, with fish tanks all over the place.

"Hey — *fish*," Carl said in wonderment.

"It's an aquarium, chucklehead," Bobbie said caustically. "What'd you expect, giraffes?"

"Look, they're feeding the sharks!" Timmy ran off to a tank across the big room.

"I wish *he* was the main course," Bobbie muttered, then shrugged off Ray's stare. "Well, go play 'Daddy,' why don't you. The sooner the kid warms up to you, the sooner we get the coins."

Ray went to join his son and found him videotaping a wolf eel. He tried to think of something to say, without success.

"If you were a fish, what kind of fish would you be?" Timmy asked, lowering his camera.

"Gee, I don't know." Ray thought. "A dolphin, maybe?"

Timmy shook his head. "A dolphin isn't a fish; it's a mammal."

"All right, all right. How about this guy?" Ray gestured toward the wolf eel, reading the description card. "Wolf eel. Bet no one messes with *him*."

"It's not really an eel, Dad," Timmy corrected him. "I'm studying about the ocean in school."

"That's nice, Tim," Ray said. "But the sign says '*wolf eel*.' I think the people who put up these signs know what they're talking about."

Timmy sighed. "Dad, is a sea horse a horse?"

"Well — no," Ray admitted, "but — "

"Is a prairie dog a dog?" Timmy asked. "And how about the L.A. Lakers? There are no lakes in Los Angeles. Why would they name their basketball team the Lakers? I rest my case." He nodded once, pleased with himself, and moved to the next tank.

Ray looked at the beady-eyed wolf eel, which looked back at him, unblinkingly.

"Just be happy you don't have kids," Ray said.

Carl and Bobbie stayed about twenty feet behind them as Timmy and his father explored the museum, talking animatedly.

"Looks like they're really getting along," Carl said, and he and Bobbie looked at each other optimistically.

Ray and Timmy stood at the cuttlefish tank not exactly "getting along."

"But it's not a fish, Dad," Timmy said.

"It is *so* a fish," Ray insisted. "It says so right there. 'Cuttle*fish*.'"

A group of schoolgirls about Timmy's age arrived, led by a beautiful female tour guide. Ray instantly smiled and winked at her.

The tour guide smiled back. "He's right, children," she said, and gestured toward Ray and Timmy. "Please continue."

"Well, thank you," Ray said, puffed up from the praise. "Like I was saying — "

"No." The tour guide shook her head, and indicated Timmy. "Him."

"Oh," Ray said, and slouched against the tank, pretending not to be embarrassed.

"It's no big thing, really," Timmy said, warming to his role as a very short educator. "As I was trying to explain to my father, the cuttlefish is actually a relative of the octopus. It's a cephalopod, not a fish."

The schoolgirls were quite impressed — and so was the tour guide.

"Very good." She smiled at Ray. "You must be terribly proud of him."

Masking his irritation with false pride, Ray patted Timmy on the shoulder. "Heh-heh. Proud ain't the word."

The tour guide and her group moved off.

To save face, Ray called after them. "By the way, that wolf eel? It's not really an eel."

The group ignored him.

"Okay, okay," he said to a smirking Timmy. "So how'd you get so smart?"

Timmy shrugged. "Beats me. Sure doesn't run in the family."

Ray stood there, bristling. Playing

"Dad" to this kid was going to be harder than he thought. He let Timmy walk off, and Bobbie and Carl joined him, as Theresa watched them from behind a guide book a few yards away.

"How're you getting along with him, Ray?" Carl asked eagerly.

"Terrific," Ray said, feigning supreme confidence. "Just terrific. By the end of today, he'll be in the palm of my hand."

It was confidence he didn't feel.

When they finally left the aquarium, Timmy was in a great mood.

"That was really fun," he said. "Next, I thought we'd all go to Alcatraz."

The three men stopped dead in their tracks. There was *no way* that they were going to go to Alcatraz.

"Maybe that's not such a good idea," Timmy said on further reflection.

The three men nodded. Visiting a prison was the *last* thing they wanted to do.

Instead, they went to an ice rink. Timmy skated around happily while peppy music played over the loudspeakers. He was holding his camcorder, and he filmed Ray, Bobbie, and Carl, who were strugging along like beginners, pathetically wobbling and falling.

Over by the ice rink's snack stand, Theresa and Alex ate candy bars and watched the action.

"Who *is* that kid?" Alex asked.

"He's Gleason's son," Theresa said confidently. "Couldn't be the other two. He's a good-looking kid." She watched Ray try to skate, her expression edging upon that of a woman seeing a handsome man, rather than a cop following a suspect.

Alex noticed this, and grinned. "Oh. Yeah. Gleason *is* good-looking. Wonder what his sign is."

Theresa looked embarrassed — and then laughed as she saw Ray fall on the ice and gamely get back up, Timmy skating literal circles around him.

They might be criminals, but they looked like they were having fun.

Chapter 14

After an hour or two of skating, Timmy and the guys went to Candlestick Park to watch a Giants game. It was "Bat Day," and in the row behind them sat a kids' baseball team, all holding bats. The kid directly behind Bobbie jumped up to cheer, accidentally dropping his bat, which hit Bobbie in the back of the head.

Bobbie whirled around. "Watch it with the bat, kid!" he snarled. "That's the second time you hit me!" He motioned toward their coach. "Hey, you! You want to rein in the brats? I'm getting pummeled here."

"Okay, kids," the coach said. "Give me your bats."

The kids groaned, but passed their bats to their coach, who was sitting on the aisle behind Timmy. The coach leaned the bats up against the outside of his seat, and the kids settled back down.

"This is great," Bobbie said grumpily. "We gotta come on Bat Day. Ten thousand kids with lethal weapons. What's next? Meat cleaver day? Uzi day?"

Timmy leaned over closer to Ray. "Do they have to come everywhere with us?"

"No," Ray said. "Tell me where you hid the stuff, and they'll go away. It'll be just you and me."

Timmy looked at him suspiciously. "If I told you where it is, then you wouldn't take me anywhere."

"Sure I would," Ray said. "You have to trust me. Give me a chance."

Timmy frowned. "The reason they're sticking with us is because they think I'll tell *you* where the stuff is — but you won't tell *them*. *They* don't trust you, why should I?"

Ray slouched down, once again trapped

in Timmy's web of logic. "You're starting to get on my nerves, you know that?"

One section over, Theresa sat watching them through a pair of binoculars. She was also eating a hot dog. She was *also* enjoying the game.

Carl, who had gone off to the snack stand, came back with his arms full of food. He squeezed past Timmy and Ray with some difficulty and sat down.

Bobbie grabbed one of the concession stand boxes and rummaged through it. "Where's my ice-cream sandwich?"

"Uh . . . under the hot dogs," Carl said.

Bobbie found what was left of the ice cream. "Terrific, it's melted. What kind of brain-dead moron puts ice cream under hot dogs?! Fine. I'll get my own." He squeezed down the row, grumbling with every step.

When he got to the end of the aisle, the crowd cheered at some action on the field, and he looked back to see what it was. As he did, he accidentally knocked Timmy's leaning bat into the kids' team's bats, causing them to fall over on the steps.

Seeing this, Timmy tried to warn him. "Uh, Bobbie — "

"Shut up, kid," Bobbie snapped. "I'm not getting you any — " He stepped on the bats and went airborne, tumbling head over heels down the cement steps and landing with a thud at the bottom. Groaning, he raised his head. "Bat Day," he said weakly.

Three more bats rolled down the steps and hit him — Bonk! Bonk! Bonk! — on the head.

Timmy, Ray, and Carl all cringed and traded pained looks.

Bobbie would have been better off if it had been Helmet Day.

When they got back to Ray's apartment, Timmy was still full of energy, but the men were exhausted. They sat slumped around the living room, Bobbie holding an ice bag on his head.

"Palm of your hand, Ray?" he said. "Palm of your hand?"

Ray shrugged defensively. "Hey, I'm doing the best I can here. Don't worry, we'll take him to a few more places, he'll loosen up, and he'll tell us."

"He better," Bobbie said darkly. "Or the

next time you see his face, it'll be on a milk carton."

In the kitchen, Timmy was on the telephone, talking loudly enough for them to hear.

"The password for today is 'bogus,' " he said. "Get that, Jason? Yeah, I'm having an *excellent* time." He listened. "Remember, I'll call you every night with a new password. And if I don't, you take that video straight to the cops. Bye, Jason."

After hanging up, he poked his head in from the kitchen.

"Better get some sleep, guys," he said with a grin. "We've got another *big* day tomorrow."

The three men groaned.

The next day, they went to a local amusement park. First, they rode the roller coaster, Timmy — who was having the time of his life — sitting up front with a white-knuckled Ray. Behind them, Bobbie and Carl were just concentrating on keeping their breakfasts down.

When the ride was over, Timmy and all the other kids came off the ride happy and smiling. Ray, Bobbie, and Carl stumbled off, glassy-eyed and wobbly legged, looking as if they'd just completed the Bataan Death March.

They rode the bumper cars next, with Ray, Carl, and Bobbie looking a little ridiculous as they tried to maneuver their tiny cars. Timmy drove like a madman, pumping his fist in the air each time he managed to rear-end one of them.

From there, they went to a photo booth, where Timmy poked his head through a large plywood figure painted to look like a Keystone Cop. Beside him, Ray bent down and put his head through a jailbird figure in prison stripes, while Carl filmed them with Timmy's camcorder.

Standing at a nearby popcorn stand, Theresa watched this whole scene, very amused.

The day passed in a dizzying montage of rides as they went from Whiplash to Shock Wave, to Death Trap, and on to Terrorizer, Panic Attack, and Mindbender. Timmy had a great time, while Ray and his friends gritted their teeth and paid money to be violently jolted, spun around, drenched in water, and whirled upside down.

They passed a booth where the San Francisco Police were holding a fundraiser, and Timmy paused when he saw the large crowd that had gathered. Many of them were police officers, both in, and out of, uniform.

"Okay, come on, who's next?" the master of ceremonies asked through a hand-held microphone. "Let's support our police department."

Timmy's hand shot up. "We'll do it!"

"No, Tim!" Ray tried to yank it back down. "*No!*"

"Ah," the master of ceremonies said happily. "Some volunteers!"

The cops surrounding them applauded.

"No way, Ray," Bobbie said in a panic. "I'm not getting up there. I'm *not* doing this."

Timmy smiled, knowing that he had leverage here. "Come on, guys. We don't want to disappoint the cops — *do* we?"

The crowd vociferously urged them on as the men traded "We're dead" looks.

They had no choice.

After they were herded up onto the stage and dressed unwillingly in costumes, a Motown song came on. Timmy, wearing a gold lamé jacket, black ducktail wig, and wraparound sunglasses, began to rip into the song, lip-synching to Wilson Pickett's gravelly voice.

On cue, Ray, Bobbie, and Carl spun around, each wearing a sixties-era beehive wig. Seeing them, the crowd laughed with delight. The men felt humiliated, but it was too late to back out now, and they grudgingly played along.

Imitating the Supremes, they clumsily tried to duplicate the backup singer's dance moves.

Watching from the edge of the crowd, Theresa laughed, having an absolutely great time.

As the song continued, the men's choreography actually started to improve. Carl was really getting into it, and suddenly, it was a contest among the three men to see who was the best.

The crowd cheered, loving every minute of it.

After their "performance," Timmy took the guys on more rides — like Speed Demon and Shock Therapy. Whenever the ride was over, he would jump off and run to the next one while Ray, Bobbie, and Carl staggered along after him.

"Come on!" Timmy said, pointing at a neon flashing sign up ahead of them.

" 'Exterminator'?" Bobbie said, and moaned. "Ray — no — not another ride!"

Timmy grinned at him, as chipper as ever. "You guys are looking a little stressed. You're not wussing out, are you?"

Ray and Bobbie were about to surrender, but Carl spoke up, in a macho show of strength.

"You kidding?" he said. "We can go on all night."

"Great," Timmy said. "Let's go get *exterminated*."

Bobbie and Ray both groaned.

They could hardly wait.

Chapter 15

When they got home, Ray collapsed on the couch, practically catatonic. Bobbie stood at the window, flicking his lighter on and off, while Carl came out of the kitchen, his arms laden with snack foods.

"You know, Ray," he said with his mouth full. "Since your kid moved in, you really started to get some great food here. I think he's a good influence."

Ray lifted his head. "Shut up, Carl," he said, and fell down again.

In the kitchen, Timmy was talking to his friend Jason on the phone.

"Jason, the password for today is 'psycho,' " he said, and then laughed. "Yeah, it's going great. I wish it would go on *forever*."

In the living room, Bobbie and Ray bit their fists so they wouldn't scream.

Later, they all sat in the kitchen and played poker, using the pennies from the big jar on Ray's dresser. Naturally, Timmy won hand after hand, the men throwing down their cards in disgust.

When the game was over, Timmy went in to lie on his father's bed. He was using colored pens to draw something on a sheet of paper. He finished his drawing by making a large "X" with a black felt pen. Then he nodded, satisfied that he had completed his task.

All in all, it had been a very successful day.

In the morning, they went fishing. Timmy stood at the shoreline, trying to cast, but could only get his line a few feet out.

"Hasn't anyone taught you to cast before?" Ray asked.

"No," Timmy said. "My father was usually in jail."

Ray was able to push the accusation aside, coming over to demonstrate proper casting technique. He stood behind Timmy and clamped his hand over his son's on the pole handle.

"Like this . . . back at one o'clock, and — " Ray snapped his wrist forward, making a good cast out into the water.

Timmy was impressed. "Wow, did *your* dad teach you that?"

Ray's face crumpled a little as he deflected a series of bad childhood memories. "No, Tim," he said finally. "He didn't."

Timmy thought about that. "I guess your family was dysfunctional, too. That's what we are — you and me. We're dysfunctional."

"You've been watching too much Oprah," Ray said, and cast again.

A few yards away, Carl fished, too — an incongruous sight, standing there in a double-breasted Armani suit and Italian loafers and holding a fishing pole. Behind him, Bobbie paced back and forth, sucking on a cigarette, raging to himself.

"Only one way to handle this," he muttered. "Only one way. I gotta get that kid alone — just once. Then I'll *make* him talk."

Carl whipped his pole back to cast, hooking the lure in Bobbie's earlobe by accident. Unknowing, Carl snapped the pole forward and Bobbie screamed.

Watching discreetly from a nearby bench, Theresa winced, cupping her hand to her own ear.

Timmy and Ray looked over as Bobbie unhooked the lure and then jumped around shouting, "Ow! Ow! Ow!"

"We're dysfunctional," Timmy said, "but *they're* stupid."

Ray laughed, shook his head, and cast.

Later, they went to the Natural History Museum. They wandered around the African Safari room and ended up in front of the zebra diorama.

"Look, Dad, Grevy's zebra," Timmy said. "It's an endangered species."

"Yeah, Ray," Carl chimed in. "That means it's threatened with extinction."

Timmy smiled at him. "That's good, Carl. That's really good."

Carl smiled back.

They walked on, leaving Bobbie looking up at the red "ENDANGERED" sticker on the diorama window.

"Endangered species," he murmured, and pictured Timmy, frozen in a diorama of his own.

"I'll be right back, Dad," Timmy said, and headed for the rest room.

Sensing his chance, Bobbie slipped away and followed him.

As Timmy walked down the hallway, he noticed this, but kept walking, not letting on that he knew he was being followed. Inside the rest room, a man was washing his hands at the row of sinks, but the room seemed to be empty otherwise.

Timmy needed a plan — fast.

Bobbie came in a couple of minutes later and knelt to tie his shoes, spotting a pair of kid's sneakers in one of the stalls. The man washing his hands dried them and left.

Bobbie waited to be sure he was gone, then swung open the stall door.

"All right, weasel!" he said. "You're telling me — " He stared, realizing that the boy *wasn't* Timmy.

"Dad! Help!" the boy yelled. "There's a guy in here!"

The large man who had been washing his hands rushed back in.

"Whoa, hey," Bobbie said, backing up. "I made a mistake, I — "

Without hesitating, the man slugged him.

Inside the *other* stall, crouching up on the toilet so he couldn't be seen, Timmy stifled a laugh.

They went from the museum off to a batting cage, so Timmy could work on his hitting. He swung and missed. Ray was standing just outside the cage, watching.

"You're uppercutting," Ray said. "Level swing. Watch the ball hit the bat."

Timmy did as he was told and hit a crisp line drive. He turned to beam at Ray, who nodded and pumped an encouraging fist in the air.

Bobbie, looking as if he was a couple of

yards short of a nervous breakdown, came up to Ray.

"You know what I think?" he asked. "I think you're starting to *like* playing Dad. That's what I think!"

"Listen, I'm just doing what the kid wants," Ray said in a low voice. "I'm playing my role, Bob. Why don't you calm down, go home, and drink some warm milk. You look terrible."

Bobbie nodded. "That's what you'd like, isn't it? Get me out of the way so you and Carl can have the coins to yourselves!"

Ray plucked the cigarette from his friend's mouth. "Filtered cigarettes, Bob," he said. "The lack of nicotine is causing brain fade. Better go back to the hard stuff." He broke off the filter and stuck the cigarette rakishly back in Bobbie's mouth.

Bobbie glared at him, flicked the cigarette away, and stormed off.

Timmy watched him go, wishing that he would never come back.

After finishing up at the batting cage, they went over to the miniature golf course.

Timmy paused at the first tee before swinging. "How about we make this interesting," he said.

Bobbie scowled, leaning on his too-short golf club. "Just hit the ball, you little rodent. I'm tired of your stupid games."

Timmy shrugged. "Okay. I was just going to say that if anybody beats me, I'll tell you where the coins are. But, if you don't want to do that. . . . "

The men exchanged significant glances.

"Hold it, hold it," Ray said. "Are you saying if any one of us beats you, you tell us where the — "

Timmy nodded. "That's what I said. And if *I* win — "

They all groaned, wondering what the catch was.

"What?" Bobbie asked snappishly. "We gotta take you to Paris tonight?"

"No," Timmy said. "Baskin-Robbins."

The men looked at each other.

"You're on," they said.

Chapter 16

The men took the game *very* seriously, playing as if it were the final round of the Masters. They cheered loudly, jumping up and down and slapping high fives when they made a putt and shouting with anguish when they missed one. All of this drew the stares of families who wondered why these grown men were so worried about this little game.

Timmy coolly made long putt after long putt. Bobbie and Ray were also playing well, keeping close on his heels. Carl, on the other hand, was a disaster.

At Hole Four, the little red schoolhouse,

Bobbie hit the ball up the incline, and it rolled back down. Carl made a "watch me do it" gesture, took a mighty swing, and — POW! — the ball rocketed up and smashed the window of the schoolhouse.

At another hole, Carl teed up a ball, swung wildly, and the ball went flying. A kindly old man was sitting on a bench near a pond with his wife, who was looking away when the ball conked the old man in the head and sent him falling backwards off the bench into the water. The wife looked back and wondered where her husband had gone. Acutely embarrassed, Carl ducked behind a bush to hide.

It was almost dusk, and they were playing at a pirate ship hole.

"He's three strokes up and we're running out of holes," Bobbie said. "You had to blow the last one. You could've gotten the ball *in* the clown's mouth."

"What about that windmill hole?" Ray wanted to know. "You took a *six* on that."

Timmy was standing with Carl, up by the tee.

"Try and hit your ball in there, through the center of the pirate ship," he said.

Carl put down his ball and aimed his putt.

"When pirates buried the stuff they stole — you know how they found it later?" Timmy said casually. "They had a treasure map."

"Uh-huh," Carl said, not really listening. He putted — and sent the ball right through the ship. "I did it!"

"Terrific," Bobbie said. "Par the last two holes, you might break a hundred and twenty." He put on an oily smile. "Now it's the lad's turn. Don't be nervous, son."

As Timmy started to swing, Bobbie cleared his throat violently in his ear — and Timmy's ball ricocheted off the pirate ship and into a pond.

"Must be the night air," Bobbie said, retrieving the ball for him. "Let's see: one stroke, another for going in the water. You're hitting *three* now, laddie."

Timmy looked at his father, disappointed that they would use such dishonest methods to beat him. Ray coughed and looked away.

At the last hole Timmy made a long putt, and Bobbie gnashed his teeth. Ray's ball, five feet from the cup, was the only one left.

"Make that, and you win, Dad," Timmy said. "Just think how much this putt is worth. All that money . . ."

"Shut up, kid!" Bobbie said. "If you're trying to psyche him out, it won't work." He turned to coach Ray. "No problem, Ray. Right in the hole."

"Easy stroke, Ray," Carl agreed. "You can do it."

Ray stood over the ball, concentrating, the tension building in all of them. He putted and the ball rolled straight for the cup, around the rim — and away.

Bobbie dropped to his knees, pounded the green with his fists, and wailed like a baby. "No! No! No! We were close, *that* close. Augghhh!"

A family at a nearby hole watched this display, shaking their heads.

"Some people take this game *way* too seriously," the father remarked.

Bobbie suddenly realized that everyone was staring at him.

"What are you looking at?" he demanded.

"I like winning, that's all! Anything wrong with that?" He threw down his putter and stalked away.

"I guess I've improved since last time we played," Timmy said to Ray. "You probably don't remember."

"Your fifth birthday," Ray said without hesitating. "I took you and nine other little boys for miniature golf and pizza." He grinned. "Compared to *that*, prison was a picnic."

Timmy laughed, too, and it was clear that there was a growing respect between them.

"Well, come on," Ray said, pretending to be gruff. "You want ice cream or not?"

"I want ice cream," Timmy said, and ran to catch up with him.

On the way to the car, Bobbie and Carl lagged behind. Bobbie was still ranting and raving about the game.

"One lousy little putt," Bobbie said, over and over. "*Why* did it come out? Why? Well, I'll tell you *this* — I'm through being bossed around by that kid. Through!"

Carl stopped, remembering something significant. "Treasure map . . . "

Bobbie stopped, too.

"When pirates buried their treasure, they made a map," Carl said slowly. "The kid said it while we were playing. Something about a treasure map."

Bobbie's eyes widened as he grasped the importance of that. "Treasure map? You think he . . . ?"

"Made a map to where the coins are!" Carl said.

Bobbie clapped his hand over Carl's mouth so Ray wouldn't hear.

Carl pried the hand off. "We have to tell Ray — "

"No!" Bobbie said, and then lowered his voice. "We keep this to ourselves. We'll check it out first. *Don't* tell Ray."

Carl nodded uncertainly.

In the parking lot, in the unmarked police car, Alex was behind the wheel, napping. Theresa saw the guys getting into Ray's car and pushed Alex's arm.

"Wake up," she said. "They're moving."

Alex cracked one eye open, and smiled dreamily. "Morning, honey . . . "

"You *wish*," Theresa said. "Start the car!"

Now fully awake, Alex turned on the ignition and pulled out after Ray's car.

In the backseat, Bobbie leaned forward.
"Ray, why don't you drop me and Carl back at your place," he suggested. "We're a little bushed."

Timmy looked surprised. "Don't you want to get ice cream?"

"*I* do," Carl said.

Bobbie threw him a swift "shut up" look. "Nah, you two go along. I guess that golf game really took it out of us, huh?" He gave Timmy a friendly pat on the shoulder, then sat back.

Ray frowned and glanced back at them in the rearview mirror. Obviously, they were up to something — he just wasn't sure what it was.

When Ray let them off at his building, Carl tried to hide a guilty expression. He would have been much happier if they told Ray about the map.

"See you two later," Bobbie said, sounding very jovial.

"What do you guys have going?" Ray asked suspiciously.

Carl started to say something, but Bobbie cut him off.

"Nothing, Ray," he said. "Just going to hang around here. Watch some TV. You don't mind, do you?"

"Come on, Dad," Timmy said, getting impatient. "Let's go, okay?"

"Yeah, go ahead," Bobbie said, nodding. "See you back here."

Despite some gnawing suspicions, Ray drove off.

"I wanted ice cream," Carl said wistfully.

Bobbie shoved him toward the steps. "Just come on. We don't have much time."

Chapter 17

As Ray drove, he was so busy worrying that he had trouble paying attention to the road.

"All of a sudden, they're not sticking to us like ticks anymore," he said, thinking aloud. "Like they trust me. Did you tell them anything?"

Timmy shrugged. "Only that they shouldn't worry about me telling you where the hiding place is. I promised I'd do it when we were all together."

Ray's eyebrows went up. "And they *bought* that?"

"Guess so," Timmy said. "Now they don't need to come with us everywhere."

Ray smiled, believing that he had the upper hand now. Against all odds, this was all going to work out fine.

At the apartment, Bobbie searched Ray's bedroom like a starving man hunting for food. He dug through drawers, tore apart the closet, and rifled Timmy's suitcase.

"Gotta be here somewhere," he mumbled. "Little weasel thinks he can outsmart me. . . . If he was *my* kid, I'd — "

"Hey, look what I found," Carl said, holding up the mattress.

There was a folded square of paper on the box spring, and Bobbie pounced on it as if it were gold. Feverishly, he unfolded the paper, revealing a maze of dotted lines, written clues, and symbols representing key points of reference. All of this led to a big "X" in the lower left corner.

"That's it!" Bobbie said triumphantly. "X marks where he hid the coins." Then he frowned. "But it's all in some kind of code."

"Can you figure it out?" Carl asked.

Bobbie snorted. "Of course I can. He's a stupid kid — you think he can outsmart me?"

"He *is* in the ninety-fifth percentile, Bob," Carl reminded him.

"What's that supposed to mean?" Bobbie asked, looking offended.

"I think it means he can outsmart you," Carl said.

Bobbie ignored that, folding up the map. "I got that little punk's number now. When he's with Ray tomorrow, *we* go on a treasure hunt."

Carl looked worried, not liking the sound of that. "What about Ray?"

Bobbie had every intention of cutting Ray out if he could, but he decided to lie to Carl. "Look, we find the coins, and Ray gets his cut like everyone else," he said. "But if we tell him we got this map, he'll want to come along — and the kid could get suspicious, maybe switch hiding places. So we're going to *keep* this to ourselves, all right?"

That made sense to Carl, and he nodded,

relieved that they weren't going to cheat their partner.

"But we can't take the original, because the kid would know we found it," Bobbie said. "So I've got to make a copy."

"Drugstore on the corner's got a machine," Carl said helpfully.

Bobbie nodded, heading for the door.

"And hey," Carl called after him. "Bring back some ice cream!"

Theresa and Alex parked their unmarked car across from the ice cream parlor. There was a light rain falling, and they peered through the windshield at Ray and Timmy, who were sitting at a table in the front window.

"So why are they taking the boy everywhere they go?" Theresa asked.

Alex shrugged, still bored by this assignment. "Maybe he's the brains of the outfit."

Theresa stared at Timmy, her mind busy at work, considering all the possibilities. "Or maybe he's got something on them," she said thoughfully. "Let's take separate cars tomorrow, in case they split up again."

Before Alex had a chance to argue, a voice came over their police radio.

"Ceranski, we've got the handoff," Detective Zinn said, his voice distorted slightly by the radio.

Theresa and Alex both looked out at the street as another unmarked car cruised past, holding Detectives Zinn and Chapman. Detective Zinn gave them a little wave of acknowledgment as they drove by and parked about half a block away.

"It's about time, Zinn," Alex said into the radio handset. Then he clicked off and looked at Theresa, not quite meeting her eyes. "So, uh — you want to go somewhere? Get a drink or something?"

"I'm busy," Theresa said, looking at Timmy.

Alex coughed to cover his embarrassment. "Hey, I wasn't asking you for a *date* or anything. All I said — "

Theresa nodded, only partially paying attention. "I know what you said. But I'm busy."

"Right. Fine," Alex said, and abruptly turned on the ignition so they could go.

* * *

In the ice cream shop, Timmy methodically worked on a large hot fudge sundae. Across the table from him, Ray drummed his fingernails against his coffee cup, trying to figure out a new angle to get out of this whole mess.

"So, Tim," he said. "You've had a pretty good time these last few days, haven't you? You can't say I haven't kept up *my* part of the bargain. No, sir, you can't say that."

Timmy stopped eating, waiting for the proverbial other shoe to drop.

Ray gave him a wide smile. "So I was thinking. . . . Maybe we could go get the coins tonight. Get that out of the way, clear the decks, so we don't have to worry about it anymore."

Timmy gave that notion some consideration, but then shook his head. "That's not our deal, Dad. Our deal is for the whole *week*."

Ray visibly deflated as he sat hunched over his coffee cup.

"But what if we do this," Timmy said, relenting slightly. Maybe it was time to suggest the idea he'd had in the back of his head all along. "What if we gave the coins back?"

Ray's mouth dropped open in surprise. "Gave the coins *back*?"

Timmy nodded, warming to the idea even more now that he had actually brought himself to say it aloud. "Yes, see, I've been thinking, Dad," he said, sounding more serious than he looked, with hot fudge dripping off his spoon. "If I tell you where the coins are, you're going to get caught."

Ray looked confused. "Caught? What're you talking about?"

Somehow, Timmy had a feeling his father knew exactly what he was talking about. "You *always* get caught, Dad. You're not a good thief. I mean — get real."

Ray flared up, stung by the criticism. "Look, don't you worry about me getting caught," he said harshly. "I've got this planned, okay? I mean, I did until *you* showed up."

Timmy looked down at his melting sundae, his feelings hurt.

Ray was going to apologize, but he wasn't quite sure how to do it, so he just hunched back over his coffee without speaking.

"I'm tired of lying to my friends," Timmy said quietly. " 'Where's your dad?' 'How come he never comes to see you?' 'Oh, he's in the CIA; he's on a secret mission somewhere.' " Timmy shook his head, remembering all the different lies he'd had to tell over the years. "I couldn't tell them where you *really* were. It's embarrassing."

Ray's expression hardened. "Oh, so I embarrass you? Well, how about when I own my own bakery? Is *that* going to embarrass you?"

"I'll always know how you got it," Timmy said, his voice very low.

There was a long, unpleasant silence.

"Whoever gets those coins is going to get caught," Timmy said. "I don't want it to be you."

Ray slammed his fist against the table. Timmy was unable to keep himself from flinching. "Now, listen, Tim," he said through gritted teeth. "We've got a deal here. I give you what you want, then *you* give me what *I* want. Are we clear on that?"

143

Timmy slumped in his chair, coming to the unhappy realization that all his hopes of having a close relationship with his father were going to be dashed — *again*. "You'll never change," he said sadly.

"I'm *trying* to," Ray said, "if you'd just cooperate."

Defiantly, Timmy grabbed his backpack and stood up. "Well, maybe I won't."

"Sit down, Tim," Ray said impatiently.

"Forget it!" Timmy shouted, and ran out of the ice cream shop into the rain and darkness.

As far as he was concerned, if he *never* saw his father again — it would be too soon.

144

Chapter 18

Ray sat alone at the table for a minute, then shook his head and dug into his pocket for money to pay the tab. Parenting was a lot more work then he had ever realized. Then he went outside, looking both ways up and down the deserted sidewalk. Timmy was nowhere in sight.

It was raining much harder than it had been before, and he let out a tired breath. It was a lousy night for Timmy to decide to run away.

"This is *all* I need," he said, and hustled over to his car so he could go look for him.

*　　*　　*

Down the street, Detectives Chapman and Zinn were watching all of this with a certain amount of confusion. They knew they were supposed to watch Ray, but if Timmy was part of it, they should stay with him, too.

"What's going on?" Zinn asked.

Chapman shrugged. "The kid was running — maybe they had an argument."

Zinn shrugged, too, and sat back to see what was going to happen next.

Timmy ran blindly through the rain, tears blurring his vision even more. He was in a fairly run-down part of town, and he bolted down the sidewalk past graffiti-covered buildings and seedy-looking street people.

If he had been less upset, he might have been scared, but right now he didn't care *what* happened.

In the meantime, Ray drove around the neighborhood, his anger now mixing with worry. Timmy might be very smart for his age, but he *was* still a kid, and this was a dangerous area of the city.

He drove up one street and down the next, getting more and more frantic, his stomach churning with anxiety.

If anything happened to his son, he would never forgive himself.

Timmy ran through the slum, his sneakers slipping and sliding on the rain-soaked streets. As he rounded a corner, he slammed smack-dab into a couple of street toughs.

"Whoa!" one of them said, holding his hands out to stop Timmy. "Where you running to, boy?"

Timmy tried to dodge out of the way, but they stepped in front of him, blocking his path.

The bigger street tough gave him a malicious smile. "What'cha got in that pack there?"

Timmy held his backpack more tightly. "Nothing," he said. "I have to get home."

The guy grabbed his pack, but Timmy gamely hung on, even as he was yanked off his feet.

"Ooh, he's a fighter, ain't he?" one of the street toughs said, and both of the men laughed, enjoying the struggle.

"Let go! It's mine!" Timmy yelled, hanging on for all he was worth.

Suddenly, the street tough was grabbed from behind and shoved away.

"Hey! Leave him alone!" Ray said furiously. "Go on, clear out of here! And you" — he pointed at Timmy — "get in the car!"

Without warning, the bigger street tough kicked Ray in the stomach, doubling him over. As the street tough laughed, Ray exploded upwards, nailing him with a thunderous punch to the face. The other punk waded into the fray, and Ray hit the guy with a short, powerful one-two combination that sent the punk sprawling onto the wet sidewalk.

As the two toughs slowly got up, Ray grabbed a trash can to clobber them, but they backed away, holding their hands up in surrender.

"Take off!" Ray yelled.

The two toughs fled, limping and hurt, neither of them looking back.

Breathing heavily, Ray put down the trash can, and rubbed his hand across his aching stomach.

Timmy just stood there, agog from witnessing the way his father had dispatched *two* thugs at once.

"Are you all right, Dad?" he asked.

"Get in the car," Ray ordered, in no mood to take any more grief from *anyone*.

"I'm sorry," Timmy said. "I really — "

Ray glared at him. "Get. In. The. *Car*," he said, enunciating each word so that his meaning could not possibly be mistaken.

Not about to argue, Timmy got in the car.

Ray stood in the alley for a few seconds, trying to catch his breath, and then gave the trash can a hard kick and got into the car himself.

He sat with both hands gripping the wheel, trying to get control of himself. It had been a long time since he'd been in a fight like that.

Timmy looked at him with newfound admiration.

"So, what're we doing tomorrow, Dad?" he asked brightly.

Ray swiveled in his seat to scowl at him, but then couldn't keep back a wry laugh as Timmy grinned at him.

"Truce?" Timmy asked.

Ray nodded slowly. "Truce," he said.

Chapter 19

Later that night, Theresa went to a noisy bar that was a hangout for off-duty cops. She was meeting Detective MacReady for a drink, and they sat up at the bar. Since Theresa never really thought of herself as being "off-duty," she was carrying a text-book, *Crime Scene Procedures*, which she set on the bar next to her.

Alex was over at the jukebox, but Theresa made a point of ignoring him as she faced straight ahead on her bar stool.

"So, you going to go out with him?" Detective MacReady asked.

Theresa shook her head so that her hair

would move back out of her face. "Who?"

"Ceranski," MacReady said, grinning. "I hear he's got the hots for you." She looked over at the jukebox. "He *is* kind of cute."

Theresa shrugged. "You think he's so cute, why don't *you* go out with him?"

"Because he doesn't want to go out with me," MacReady said. "He wants to go out with you. And he's heading this way." She stood up, still grinning. "I'll just leave you two alone."

Theresa rolled her eyes at that and picked up her textbook, pretending to read.

Alex approached her somewhat tentatively. "Thought you were busy."

Theresa nodded, reading. "I am."

Alex took the book from her and squinted to read the title. "*Crime Scene Procedures.* I read this once." He winked at her. "I won't tell you how it ends."

Theresa took the book back and resumed reading.

Alex shifted his weight uncomfortably, then tried a different tack to engage her. "You know, Walsh, you have to learn to relax, let your hair down. Just because your dad was the greatest cop in the solar system doesn't mean you have to be just like him twenty-four hours a day."

Theresa turned a page in her book.

Alex picked up her drink and sniffed it. "7Up," he said, and put the glass down. "How about I buy you a *real* drink?"

Theresa turned another page. "No, thanks."

Alex let out his breath, starting to get frustrated. "Hey, I'm just trying to break the ice here, you know? What's going on? What'd I ever do to you, huh?"

Theresa sighed, and lowered her book. "Just stop treating me like" — she tried to think of the right word — "like I don't know what I'm doing. I can do the job, Ceranski. I can *do* it."

Alex cocked an eyebrow, since that last part had sounded more as if she had been trying to convince *herself*. "The lieutenant's the one to convince, not me," he said. "But I could give you some help."

Theresa was tired of him trying to "help" her, so she read her book, ignoring him.

Alex looked at her lovely profile, well aware that she didn't want his advice. But he decided to give it to her anyway.

153

"When you're working surveillance, how about trying to fit in, dress like other" — he hesitated, not sure how she would take the compliment — "attractive women your age, not like a cop. And, especially, get rid of those *shoes*." He shook his head and walked away to join a rowdy group of other cops from their precinct.

Theresa looked down at her clunky sensible shoes and frowned. Much as she hated to admit it — he might be right.

The next morning, Ray stood at the bathroom sink, holding the toothpaste. Opening the medicine cabinet, he looked around for his toothbrush, but he didn't find it.

"Where's my toothbrush?" he asked, and bent down to check underneath the sink.

Timmy stuck his head in the door. "I threw it out, Dad."

Ray looked up, bumping his head on the bottom of the sink. "You *what*?"

"The bristles were all matted and stuff," Timmy said, and went over to the toothbrush holder, where two new toothbrushes — one red, and one green — were hanging. "You're supposed to change your toothbrush every three months. Didn't you know that?" He slapped the green toothbrush into Ray's hand and left.

Ray looked down at his new toothbrush and sighed. Was there *anything* in the world that his son didn't know?

After breakfast, they went to play basketball in the park.

"You know, a toothbrush is a personal thing," Ray said, as they walked down the street. "And *I'll* decide when mine's expired."

"But the bristles were matted," Timmy said.

"I don't care if the bristles were matted," Ray answered, somewhat childishly. "I *like* matted bristles."

"Well, maybe we can run over your new one with the car," Timmy suggested. "Would that make you happy?"

"It might," Ray said, and grinned.

They were walking past a bakery — one of Ray's competitors — and he paused to examine the big wedding cake in the window.

"Now look at that," he said, shaking his head.

Timmy shrugged. "It's a cake."

"Look at the crummy detail work on that frosting," Ray said, pointing. "I wouldn't give that cake to Hitler." He shook his head, completely disgusted. "People who ruin baked goods like that should be *arrested*."

Across the street, Theresa was loitering by a newsstand as she browsed through magazines. Despite all of her inbred cop instincts, she had taken Alex's advice and dressed with a little more care that morning. She had selected more fashionable heels, a shorter skirt, and was even wearing makeup.

In a purely nonprofessional way, she kind of hoped her new outfit *didn't* make her blend into the woodwork.

Ray and Timmy went into the park and started playing a casual game of one-on-one on a playground court. Ray dribbled twice and shot a twenty-footer, which swished cleanly through the net.

"Whoa," Timmy said. "Not bad."

"Not bad?" Ray trotted in to get the rebound. "I was second team all-conference in high school."

Timmy looked impressed. "I didn't know that."

"There's a lot of things you don't know," Ray said, and dribbled to the top of the key while Timmy guarded him. Ray stopped dribbling. "Like how to guard someone. Get your hands up, and get on the balls of your feet."

Timmy put his hands up, doing his best to guard Ray.

"How come you didn't go to college?"

Ray faked left and dribbled to the right. Timmy was barely keeping up. "Because I had to get a job first," he said. "I was working at a loading dock for eighty-nine fifty a week, trying to save for college. One day, a guy comes to me and says, 'Want to earn five hundred bucks? Look the other way when our truck backs up.'" He shrugged, and hit another twenty-footer.

Timmy let his arms fall, visibly disappointed.

"I'm not making excuses," Ray said. "I

needed the money and I took a short cut."

Timmy nodded. "Just like you're doing now."

"Yeah," Ray conceded, "but this is the last time."

Timmy shook his head and looked down at the ground. No matter what, his father just wasn't going to change.

What Timmy had to decide now was if he was ever going to be able to accept that. The simple truth was that he was starting to like Ray a whole lot more than he *disliked* him.

Chapter 20

They kept playing, Ray making almost all of his shots, and Timmy missing most of his. Ray was going over to retrieve the ball from the end of the court when two attractive women in running shorts jogged by.

"Ladies, how about a little basketball game here?" Ray said. "Some two-on-two action. Hey, it's a great calorie burner. Tim-boy, tell them. Heh-heh . . . "

The women kept on running, ignoring him.

Ray looked at Timmy. "Nice going. Some

adroit patter on your part, and we could've landed those two."

"What was I supposed to say?" Timmy asked self-consciously.

Ray stared at him. "Don't you know how to talk to girls?"

Timmy shrugged, embarrassed.

"I can't believe you're my kid," Ray said, shaking his head.

"Yeah, well, it's not something I like to brag about," Timmy shot back good-naturedly.

"Okay, okay," Ray said. "How to pick up girls. First, get them talking. Now, pretend I'm some fabulous babe you want to hit on." He adopted a feminine pose, putting his hand on his hip, and strutting around the court.

Timmy looked around, mortified. *"Dad."*

"Come on, give me a line, stranger," Ray said, and blew him a kiss.

At the newsstand, Theresa watched this silly display, wondering exactly what it was that Ray was doing.

"Come on, handsome," Ray said, prancing around. "I'm getting away here, I'm walking out of your life. . . . "

Timmy wracked his brain, trying to come up with something. "Um, um — nice basketball!"

Ray turned coquettishly. "Oh! You think so?"

"Um . . . yeah," Timmy said. "Where'd you get it?"

"Perfect, *perfect*," Ray said, back to his normal voice. "Disarm them with a compliment, follow with a question. Now you've got the lady's attention. 'So I notice you've got the Michael Jordan autographed ball there.' " He switched to a higher, feminine voice. " 'Oh, yes, Michael is my favorite player.' " He returned to his own voice. " 'Me, too. Me, too. Say, if you've got a few minutes, would you like to go for coffee?' " He went back to being the woman. " 'Oh, I thought you'd *never* ask.' " He shrugged, and dribbled the ball a few times. "See? It's that easy."

"It is?" Timmy asked doubtfully.

"Give it a shot," Ray said, and threw up a thirty-footer.

The ball slipped through the hoop with a very satisfying and successful *swish*.

Timmy got the point.

* * *

Bobbie and Carl were spending the morning trying to decipher Timmy's map. They stood in Union Square, underneath a large American flag, arguing.

"Look," Bobbie said, pointing. "The map starts at a picture of a flag, right? That has to mean *this* flag. We start *here*."

"What makes you so sure it's *this* flag?" Carl asked doubtfully.

Bobbie shrugged. "Because it's a big flag, it's near Ray's place — it *has* to be this one." He examined the map. "Okay. It says go east for seventy-five giant steps. Go ahead, count them off."

Carl started to take giant steps. "One, two, three . . . "

"Hey, hey, what are you doing?" Bobbie asked, trying to stop him. "Those are *your* giant steps. It's gotta be *kid* giant steps."

"Oh." Carl looked down at his huge, if well-shod, feet. "So how big are kid giant steps?"

They looked at each other and then frowned, perplexed by this problem.

A kid about Timmy's age came along

with his mother. They were walking their big Doberman pinscher.

"Hey, lady, let us use your kid for a minute," Bobbie said.

Afraid that she was being accosted, the mother pushed the dog toward them. "Thor — kill!" she ordered.

The dog lunged at them, barking and snarling, and Bobbie and Carl recoiled.

"Okay, okay, forget it," Bobbie said quickly. "Forget it, lady!"

Satisfied that she had disarmed these two miscreants, the woman tugged on the leash. "Good, Thor, come."

Thor broke off in mid-attack and, wagging his stumpy tail, calmly walked away with his owners.

"Boy," Bobbie said. "Ask for a little help these days, you get your head bit off." He looked at Carl. "Where were we?"

"Giant steps," Carl said.

"Yeah, yeah." Bobbie paused to think. "Okay, let's say one of your giant steps equals two of the kid's. So — " he closed his eyes, doing the math in his head. "Half of seventy-five is thirty-seven and a half.

Take thirty-seven and a half giant steps
that way."

Carl nodded, and began counting off
giant steps.

Alex, who was posted up the street in
his unmarked car, shook his head.

"I don't believe this," he said, and
slouched back in his seat, closing his eyes.

This was not the best duty assignment
he'd ever had.

Over by the playground, Theresa was
getting ready to leave the newsstand because Ray and Timmy seemed to have finished their basketball game.

Ray stopped on the street corner. "Stay
here," he said, and went off to the closest
phone booth. He fished around in his pocket
for change, and then dialed his fence.

The phone rang several times, and then
an answering machine picked up. Ray
shook his head, amused by the deadpan
"I'm not home right now" message. But,
then again, thieves had social lives, the
same as anyone else did.

"Dobbs, it's Ray," he said after the beep.

"I guess you're out. I just wanted to let you know we're set for Sunday. I've got the merchandise. No problem."

As he waited for his father to get off the phone, Timmy stood on the corner, dribbling the basketball. The ball hit his foot, bounced into the street, and he ran after it.

Theresa gasped, seeing Timmy dart into traffic — straight into the path of an oncoming bus.

"Look out!" she shouted instinctively and covered her eyes.

If he was going to be run over, she couldn't bear to see it happen.

Chapter 21

The bus roared by, cutting off her view of Timmy, and she held her breath, not sure if he had been hit. The ball rolled across the street and the bus passed, revealing Timmy standing there, unhurt, looking at her curiously. Theresa heaved a sigh of relief as the ball hit the curb at her feet.

"Can I have my ball, please?" Timmy asked.

Their eyes met, and she realized that her impulsive yell had ruined everything. He had seen her now, and that was it. Her cover was completely blown.

She wasn't sure what to do, but it was

already too late, so she decided that the only choice left was — to pick up the ball.

"Stay *right* there," she said, and stalked across the street with the basketball tucked under her arm, to read him the riot act. "Don't you know not to dart into traffic like that? You *never* run into the street without looking both ways!"

Timmy was taken aback and didn't know how to respond. "Gee, okay, I — I'm sorry," he said.

Seeing a strange woman haranguing his son, Ray hustled out of the phone booth.

"Hey, hey, what's going on here?" he asked, prepared to lose his temper.

"What's going on?" Theresa asked, having *already* lost her temper. "He ran into the street and was almost hit by a bus, *that's* what's going on."

Ray gave Timmy a harmless swat on the head. "What's wrong with you?" he asked, then looked at Theresa. "He's got a habit of running off. Good you were watching him. Thanks."

Theresa looked at him, and they both held the gaze. Ray was a handsome man and, up close, his eyes were warm and friendly. She didn't want to admit it, but she was attracted to him.

"I, uh, I wasn't *watching*. I was just crossing the street, and — well — " She gave the ball back to Timmy. "Just look both ways next time, okay?" She smiled nervously at them and started to walk away.

"Nice sweater," Timmy said, deciding to give his father's strategy for talking to women a try. "Where'd you get it?"

She stopped, thrown by the question. "Sears," she said. "I got it at Sears."

Timmy nodded. "Sears. How about that." He paused. "You want to go for coffee?"

Theresa didn't answer, at a loss for words.

Ray just grinned.

They ended up in a coffee shop farther up the block. Ray and Theresa had coffee, while Timmy ordered milk and a doughnut.

"So, what do you do, Theresa?" Ray asked.

"Um . . . " Theresa shook her head, her mind still at a loss. Maybe undercover work wasn't her destiny. "I'm a teacher. I, uh, teach kindergarten."

Ray whistled in sympathy. "*That's* got to be a tough job. You must like kids."

"Oh, yes," Theresa agreed, with genuine enthusiasm. "Children are special."

Timmy, who had two straws stuck up his nose, noisily blew bubbles into his milk, making an obnoxious sound. He saw Ray and Theresa looking at him and stopped.

"What?" he asked innocently, and took the straws out of his nose.

Theresa smiled, and changed the subject. "What line of work are you in, Ray?"

"He makes cakes," Timmy volunteered. "He decorates them."

"Oh, that's quite an art," Theresa said. "I took a class in that, once."

"So did he, when he was in — " Timmy stopped, as Ray shot him a look — "in, uh, college."

"Oh?" Theresa said, pleasantly casual. "Where'd you go?"

Ray looked at her for a minute and then decided that, for once in his life, he was going to be honest. "Folsom U," he said. "It's a state institution."

Theresa, of course, had already known this, but she feigned surprise. "Oh. You mean, um . . . the prison?"

Timmy spoke up, hoping to smooth over the awkward silence. "He didn't shoot anybody or anything. He just stole something, and — right, Dad?"

"Yeah, I stole something," Ray agreed, and gave Theresa a disarming smile. "But that was a long time ago. And you could say I'm a different man now, Theresa."

Theresa looked at him and, deep inside, a tiny part of her hoped that he was telling the truth. "Well, I'm glad to hear that," she said, and smiled back.

"We're going to the museum this afternoon," Timmy said. "Want to come with us?"

Theresa hesitated. "Well, I — "

"If you don't have anything else planned, that is," Ray said.

"Well, yeah, I don't know, I — " Theresa paused to take a breath and try to think clearly. "I did have this — thing." She was going to have to do better than "thing." "I was, um, going to meet my dentist for, um — I have a tooth that's, um — " She

170

touched her jaw reflexively, remembering to wince a little. "But it's feeling better — the tooth — so let me see if I can call and reschedule the appointment." Mentally kicking herself for fumbling around like that, she got up and headed for a pay phone in the back of the coffee shop.

"She's nice," Timmy said cheerfully. "Do you like her?"

Ray watched her walk away, wondering what it was about her that unsettled him. "I don't know. Maybe."

Theresa glanced over her shoulder to make sure neither of them had followed her and then dialed her partner on his cellular phone to bring him up to date. Somehow, she wasn't surprised when he overreacted.

"*What*?" Alex shouted. "You're supposed to tail the suspect, not *date* him."

"Look, I can't explain right now," Theresa said, cupping her hand over her mouth to be sure that Ray and Timmy wouldn't hear her conversation. "But if I can get close and get him talking — "

"Does he know you're a cop?" Alex asked.

"Of *course* not," Theresa said, insulted

that he would even suggest such a thing.

"Look," Alex said, obviously very concerned. "I don't like this."

"I can take care of myself, Ceranski," Theresa said abruptly, and hung up the phone.

She was on her own — with no backup — and she kind of *liked* it.

Chapter 22

Bobbie and Carl were still doing their best to solve the mystery of Timmy's map, although the exact size of the various steps they were supposed to take — both giant and baby — still presented a problem.

Carl walked along, barely moving his feet, as Bobbie followed, his eyes glued to the map.

". . . a hundred eighty-five," Carl counted, "hundred eighty-six, hundred eighty-seven . . ."

"Baby steps!" Bobbie said. "The map says baby steps!"

"I'm *taking* baby steps," Carl insisted.

"Hundred eighty-eight, hundred eighty-nine . . ."

They passed a street vendor who was selling leather jackets.

"Genuine leather jackets," the vendor was shouting, "fifty-nine ninety-five, only fifty-nine ninety-five!"

"Fifty-nine ninety-six," Carl counted, "Fifty-nine ninety-seven, fifty-nine — " He stopped, realizing that he had lost track. He looked at Bobbie, and they both wailed in frustration.

They were going to have to start over. *Again.*

Timmy and Ray took Theresa to the San Francisco Museum of Modern Art. The art was very — modern, to say the least.

Timmy stood in front of a painting, cocking his head from one side to the other, trying to make sense of it. The painting was a large black-and-white abstract by Franz Kline, and Timmy found it nothing if not obscure.

Ray and Theresa came over and stood next to him.

"I don't get it," Timmy said.

"It's called abstract expressionism," Theresa explained. "By Franz Kline. He's known for his bold brushwork. His use of positive and negative space."

Ray and Timmy gave her "who are *you* trying to impress?" looks.

Theresa flushed, realizing that she must have sounded a little pompous. "I, uh, had a year of art history."

Timmy shrugged and was moving on to the next painting when Ray stopped him.

"Wait a minute," he said, pulling him back. "Tell me what you see here."

Timmy shrugged again. *"Paint.* A buncha paint."

Ray nodded. "Exactly. You see, this guy Kline *wants* you to see the brush strokes. It's not some three-dimensional illusion like those other paintings we saw. It's just a *buncha* paint, Tim. That's it."

Timmy stepped back, seeing the painting with new eyes. "Oh," he said. *"Cool."*

Theresa looked at Ray, impressed by his simple, yet elegant explanation.

Ray shrugged a little self-consciously. "Had a cellmate who was an art forger," he said. "He taught me a few things."

Charmed, Theresa smiled to herself, and then broke off the smile. No matter what, she *could not* fall for this guy. She was a *professional*.

Ray brought Timmy up close to another painting, after telling him to keep his eyes closed.

"Okay, now open your eyes," he said.

Timmy did, and saw dabs of paint — crimson, violet, green. They were little dots of pure, vibrant color, put down in a seemingly haphazard fashion.

"What do you see?" Ray asked.

Timmy shrugged. "Dots. A buncha dots."

"Now close your eyes," Ray said.

Timmy closed his eyes, and Ray led him back twenty feet from the painting to where Theresa was standing, curious about what Ray was doing. Ray stopped and turned Timmy to face the painting.

"Open them," he said.

Timmy opened his eyes, and saw Georges Seurat's "An Afternoon in the Park," the magnificent wall-sized masterpiece of pointillism. It was a feast for the senses, and he stared in wonder.

"Wow," he said.

Ray nodded. "Millions of little dots, Tim. Up close, they don't look like much, but put them all together, and . . . " He looked over at Theresa. "Sometimes, at first glance, things aren't what they seem."

Timmy walked up to get a closer look at the painting.

"I guess that goes for people, too, huh?" Ray said.

Theresa hesitated, not sure where he was going with that. "Does it?"

"Like, you take cops," Ray said. "They think they have this special ability to look at you and know who you are. Once a con, always a con. But a lot of times, they're wrong." He paused, significantly. "That's one thing I don't like about cops. They assume too much."

They looked at each other for a long minute.

"I assure you, I don't make a habit of assuming," Theresa said.

Ray nodded, somewhat reassured. "Neither do I," he said.

They looked at each other and then, feeling uncomfortable, looked in opposite directions.

Timmy had gone over to another painting, where he stood next to two highbrow yuppies, who were dressed all in black. Seeing him, they both looked down at him snootily.

"Don't you just love the bold brushwork?" Timmy said. "The use of positive and negative space? How exhilarating." He moved on to the next painting, leaving the two yuppies open-mouthed.

When they had looked at enough paintings for one day, they went to the museum gift shop. As Ray browsed through the books, Theresa pretended to look through the posters. Timmy came up to her, just enjoying being next to her.

"You smell like my mother," he said. "Your perfume, I mean. What is it?"

Theresa blinked. "It's, uh, White Linen."

Timmy nodded. "She used to wear that a lot."

Theresa wasn't quite sure what to make of his use of the past tense. "Does she live in San Francisco?" she asked.

Timmy's face crumpled slightly and he swallowed, hard. "She's dead," he said after a pause. "She had cancer."

"Oh," Theresa said, feeling guilty for asking. "I'm sorry."

Timmy nodded, his hands shoved deep in his pockets, wanting to confide in her, even though they had only just met a couple of hours before. "It was three years ago," he said. "I live with my aunt in Redding now. She's nice, but she married this real dork. He doesn't even want me around." He looked over at Ray, who was still poking through coffee-table art books. "I think I'm going to move in with my dad — you know, permanently. He needs me."

As he went over to join his father, Theresa watched him, her emotions completely conflicted. On the one hand, if Ray was a thief, she wanted to bust him; on the other hand, she didn't want to see this boy's dreams go up in smoke.

For the first time in her life, she found herself wishing that she was anything *but* a cop.

Chapter 23

Carl and Bobbie had followed the map until they found themselves at the mouth of an alley, near a restaurant.

Bobbie frowned at the map. "I'm sure we did everything right," he said uncertainly.

"Maybe we didn't," Carl said. "Maybe you missed something."

Bobbie shook his head. "I didn't miss nothing! Look around."

They both looked until, finally, Bobbie glanced down the alley and saw, amid a jumble of graffiti, a faded red "X" on the brick wall.

"There!" He stabbed at the map with his forefinger. "An X. X marks the spot!"

They ran down the alley to the red "X." Directly underneath the mark, they found a large trash Dumpster.

"You think he hid it in here?" Carl asked. "Seems kind of dumb. Trash truck could come along, haul it away."

Bobbie shrugged. "So maybe the kid ain't so smart, after all."

He threw open the Dumpster lid, and they peeked inside to see flies buzzing over piles of rotting vegetables and food scraps. The stench was unbelievable, and they both turned their heads away.

"Get in and take a look," Bobbie said.

Carl shook his head, indicating his suit. "I'm not getting in there. This is a Pierre Cardin. Cost me six bills."

"A fortune at our fingertips, and you're worried about your dumb *suit*," Bobbie said, clicking his tongue in dramatic dismay.

"Well, you buy your clothes at garage sales," Carl pointed out. "*You* get in there."

Bobbie heaved an angry sigh, and

climbed into the Dumpster. "Go keep a lookout," he said.

Alex, up at the alley entrance, snuck a look around the corner just in time to see Bobbie getting into the Dumpster. He shook his head, puzzled. What were these morons *up* to, anyway?

"Oh, this is *terrible*," Bobbie said, wading around in the trash. "It stinks!" Then he screamed. "AAAGH! There's a dead rat in here! It's big as a terrier!"

Carl ambled toward the alley entrance, catching sight of a pushcart vendor selling hot pretzels across the street. Unable to resist the temptation, he ran over there to get a snack.

In the meantime, Bobbie rummaged through the garbage, swearing under his breath.

A busboy wearing Walkman headphones came out of the restaurant alley door and dumped a trash can full of disgusting-looking scraps into the Dumpster.

Bobbie was completely covered and he leaped up, enraged. "Hey!"

Not hearing him over the music playing on his Walkman, the busboy flipped the

Dumpster lid down and CLANG! — it nailed Bobbie in the head as it slammed shut.

Across the street, Carl squeezed some mustard onto his pretzel, humming to himself.

A large trash truck rumbled down the alley, approaching the Dumpster, as Bobbie groaned weakly inside. The trash truck's forklift skewered the Dumpster and started to raise it.

Bobbie lifted his groggy head, not sure what was happening. "Wha — ? Hey!"

Carl, munching his pretzel, walked back down the alley and saw the Dumpster, upside down over the top of the truck, emptying mounds of garbage — and a screaming Bobbie — into its hold. He was so surprised that he dropped his pretzel, getting a dab of mustard on his tie. He looked down at the spot, frowning.

"Darn," he said.

Timmy and Theresa walked down Fisherman's Wharf, next to the Aquatic Park. Ray was off at a popcorn stand, buying food for all of them.

"So you're a teacher, huh?" Timmy said. "My teacher, Mrs. Carver, she's fat. Not like you." He paused. "I think my dad likes you."

"Well — I like the both of you," Theresa said uncomfortably.

Timmy's face clouded. "Can I ask you a question?"

Theresa nodded. "Sure."

"If you had a secret that someone really wanted to know, but you knew if you told them it'd get them in big trouble — would you tell them the secret anyway?" Timmy asked, no longer able to keep everything to himself.

Surmising that Timmy might be divulging something about the robbery, Theresa casually picked up on her cue. "I don't know," she said. "Maybe you could tell me what the secret is, and I could tell you what I'd do."

Timmy was about to answer when Ray came over with the popcorn.

"Here you go," he said, handing boxes around.

Theresa put on a smile, masking her disappointment. She had been *so* close. "Thanks."

"No problem," Ray said, and walked Timmy out of her earshot. "What's between us is between *us*, right?"

Timmy hesitated, but then nodded. "Sure, Dad," he said, and ran off to scatter popcorn to the pigeons.

After wandering around the Wharf for a while, they went to Neiman Marcus to do some shopping. Timmy quickly made himself scarce, and Ray found himself following Theresa around the women's department.

"Where *is* that kid?" he asked impatiently. "Says we have to come here, asks me for money, then disappears."

Theresa lifted a blouse to check the price. The price was *very* high, and she put it back down. "He says he lives with his aunt," she remarked casually.

Ray nodded. "My sister. She's got a nice big house down in Redding. There're good schools. He's got all his friends. He's better off there."

Theresa glanced at him from the corner

of her eye. "He doesn't think so. He told me he'd rather live with you."

Ray was taken aback. "He said that?" He smiled to himself, unaccountably pleased. "Huh."

Timmy came running up, carrying a shopping bag.

"Hey, pal, where you been?" Ray asked.

"I bought something," Timmy said. He pulled a small gift box from the bag and handed it to Theresa. "For you. Open it."

Theresa was surprised — and very touched. "For me? Why?"

Timmy grinned at her. "I could've been roadkill today. You saved me. Come on, open it."

She unwrapped the package to find a bottle of cologne.

"It's White Linen," Timmy said to Ray. "She likes the same stuff Mom used to wear."

"I noticed," Ray said softly, and he and Theresa looked at each other.

Timmy pulled on her arm. "You can wear it tonight when we go to dinner."

Theresa blinked. Since when were they going to *dinner*?

"Next thing you know, he'll be proposing," Ray said, then cleared his throat. "So, uh, you free tonight?"

Theresa hesitated, wondering if she was getting in too deep here. She looked at Timmy, who obviously *really* wanted her to come.

". . . I'm free," she found herself saying, and was very gratified by the big grins they gave her.

As they walked down the aisle, they passed a mannequin with a Nike logo travel bag slung over its shoulder.

Timmy stopped, realizing that it was the same style and color bag that Ray had had the coins in. "Hey, that looks just like — "

"Yeah, yeah, the bag I keep my gym stuff in," Ray said, quickly cutting him off. "Kids remember the dumbest things."

He pushed Timmy forward as Theresa cast a thoughtful glance at the bag before going on.

Timmy looked back over his shoulder at the mannequin just before they turned the corner, feeling the beginnings of an idea in his brain.

Chapter 24

Standing on the sidewalk near the alley, his clothes stained and foul-smelling from the garbage, Bobbie paced maniacally back and forth.

"So maybe we took a wrong turn back there," he said. "Okay, so we retraced our steps, and it has to be here. It's *gotta* be around here."

"One thing we ain't thought about," Carl ventured. "Maybe the map don't lead anywhere. Maybe the kid made it to get us out of the way."

Bobbie looked at him, his frenzied eyes considering that awful thought — and rejecting it. "No," he said. "No, that little twerp couldn't be that vicious. He — he *couldn't*." Then something caught his gaze, and he smiled.

Across the street there was an old Catholic church. Carved in stone above the entrance was a big cross.

"Wait, it's not an X," he said and turned the map sideways so the "X" became a cross. "It's a *cross*."

They hurried across the street, sure that they had found the coins at last. Once they were inside, they stood at the back of the church.

It was a cavernous place with vaulted ceilings, an ornately decorated altar, stained-glass windows, and beautiful marble statues everywhere. The rows of ancient wooden pews were empty, and Carl stared, spooked by the holy silence.

"This place is like a 7-Eleven — it's open all night," Bobbie said, lighting a cigarette. "It's a perfect place for him to hide it."

Carl gestured toward the cigarette. "Hey, God don't allow smoking."

Bobbie shrugged and was about to put the cigarette out in the holy water font, but

Carl grabbed his hand in a viselike grip. Bobbie winced and jerked his hand free, giving Carl a dirty look as he ground the cigarette out on the floor. Then he gestured "come on," and started up the center aisle.

Carl, feeling extremely uncomfortable, followed him.

Bobbie signalled for him to look in the organ pit over on the left, while he went to check a display of votive candles. Finding nothing, Bobbie started to move away when he saw a donation box. The box was filled with coins and a few dollar bills — and it was very tempting.

Just as Bobbie reached into the donation box, Carl's hand accidentally depressed the organ keys and a loud, shrill organ blast shattered the silence. Startled, Bobbie pulled his hand away, getting singed on the candle flames. He stifled a cry of pain and shot Carl a dark look.

In the sacristy, which was the priest's dressing room off the sanctuary, a nun had heard the organ blast. She was a stout little bulldog of a woman, who was carrying two heavy brass candlesticks. She quickly went to the open doorway and saw Bobbie snatching money from the donation box.

Hastily, she set down the candlesticks, went to the nearby phone, and dialed 911.

Carl joined Bobbie reluctantly at the communion rail, and Bobbie motioned toward the figure of Christ on the cross hanging on the back wall of the sanctuary. Underneath the cross was a marble table, fringed in white satin drapery, upon which the sacraments — the holy water and wine cruets — were resting.

Carl shook his head "*no*," refusing to go up there, but Bobbie climbed over the communion rail, motioning vigorously for him to follow. With much trepidation, Carl swung his leg over the rail, looking guiltily up at the cross.

Bobbie crouched down and lifted the satin drapery, finding a sealed cardboard box under there. He smiled, and picked it up.

"Put that back!" a stern voice said.

They whirled around to see the small, stout nun brandishing a heavy candlestick like a club.

"This is a house of God!" she said, outraged.

Bobbie shrugged.

The nun swung the candlestick, just missing them. They bolted, stumbling over the communion rail and running up the center aisle as fast as they could.

"Stop, thieves!" the nun yelled after them.

Outside, two police cars roared up in front of the church. Alex, who was sitting in his unmarked car, looked up from his crossword puzzle, alarmed.

Carl and Bobbie — who was clutching the box — dashed through the church doors and down the stone steps. Then they froze, seeing three police officers standing there with their guns trained on them.

"Don't move!" one of them barked. "Hands behind your heads!"

Instinctively, Bobbie dropped the box, and it fell on the steps, breaking open. Wine bottles spilled out, shattering noisily.

Carl and Bobbie traded pained looks. They were about to be arrested for the wrong crime.

*   *   *

Theresa wasn't supposed to meet Ray and Timmy until seven o'clock, so she had time to go home first and change into her prettiest dress.

She stood in front of her mirror, brushing her hair until it flowed gracefully down her back. Then she picked up the bottle of White Linen Timmy had given her and spritzed on a little. She breathed in the scent, feeling more feminine than she had for a long time — until her eyes fell on her gun, hanging holstered on the chair.

Wrenched back to reality, her face fell. She had to remember that this wasn't a real date. She was a cop, and it was her job to *nail* this guy.

Like it or not.

They met at a small Italian restaurant and were seated at a small candlelit table. It was a very nice meal, and the three of them laughed and talked the entire time.

"I like your hair that way," Ray said as the waiter removed their plates. "Looks pretty."

"Thank you," Theresa said shyly, and took a sip of wine. Remembering what her job was, she switched gears, delicately probing. "So, Ray. You like where you're working? You plan to stay there?"

Ray nodded. "Yeah. In fact, I might even buy the place."

Theresa felt her heart sink, but she forced a smile. "That's great," she said. "If you don't mind my asking, how do you get financing for that? Do you get a small business loan?"

"Yeah, a loan. I'm kind of waiting for that to come through," Ray said, and glanced covertly at Timmy.

Theresa looked down, wishing that she hadn't seen the glance.

The maître d' appeared at the table and whispered something into Ray's ear. He nodded, and the man bowed and left.

"The Dodgers are coming in next week, Dad," Timmy said. "You think we could go?"

Ray looked at him, realizing that, in an oblique way, Timmy was asking if he could stay with him — permanently. But before he could answer, he was interrupted by the sound of voices singing, "Happy Birthday."

They all turned to see a large rectangular birthday cake, glowing with lit candles, being carried to their table by a group of beaming waiters.

The other diners in the restaurant applauded.

Timmy looked at his father in confusion because it *wasn't* his birthday.

"Just say it's for all the birthdays I missed, Tim," Ray said. "Sorry I couldn't make the cake myself."

For once, Timmy was speechless. He looked from his father, to the cake, to Theresa, trying to figure out if this could really be happening.

"Well, come on," Ray said. "Make a wish and blow out the candles — before the fire sprinklers come on."

Timmy looked first at Ray then at Theresa, and closed his eyes, making a wish that was very easy to guess. He took a big breath and blew out the candles, everyone in the restaurant clapping again. Theresa smiled and reached over to squeeze his hand lightly, and Timmy's face widened into an even bigger grin.

Ray took the knife from the waiter and addressed the room in general. "I doubt my son can eat all of this — so, who wants a piece?"

The rest of the diners laughed and raised their hands. Theresa and Timmy laughed, too, and Timmy tried to help as Ray started to cut the cake.

No one looking at their smiling table would ever guess that they were anything other than a very happy and loving family.

Chapter 25

After dinner, they went to the Palace of Fine Arts park. It was a warm, magical summer night, with romance in the air. A band was playing as couples strolled under the stars and children — including Timmy — ran around, waving sparklers.

Ray and Theresa walked together, close enough to hold hands, had they been so inclined.

"So, why'd you become a teacher?" Ray asked.

Theresa was glad that it was dark and he couldn't see her expression. "My dad was a teacher. I never wanted to be anything else."

"That's good," Ray said admiringly. "You knew what you wanted and you went for it. I wasn't sure what I wanted. So — I became a thief."

"But you're not a thief anymore," Theresa both said and asked.

"Yeah." Ray looked tense. "That's right."

They walked for a few minutes without speaking.

Ray let out his breath, knowing that she deserved a better explanation than that. "Of course, I said the same thing to my ex-wife when we got married. And then when Timmy was five, I got arrested again and went to jail." He stopped, shaking his head. "She never forgave me for that. Said if I didn't love them enough to stay out of jail — then I didn't love them enough. And the best thing I could do was just to get out of their lives. Don't write. Don't call. Just be dead, you know?" He shook his head again. "So I was."

A spray of fireworks exploded over the

park and Ray looked at Timmy, who was tracing the night with his sparkler.

Theresa watched him look fondly at his son.

"I guess you have to decide," she said. "What you want. What's most important."

Their eyes met, and he surprised her by leaning forward and giving her a kiss. She was also surprised when she found herself kissing *back*.

The only person who was even *more* surprised was Alex, who was standing in the shadows, watching. He shook his head, very troubled by what his partner was doing.

Theresa pulled away from Ray, shaky and out of breath. Her heart wanted to give in to this man, but her head wrenched her back from the brink.

"I'm sorry," Ray said. "Was that wrong?"

"No, but — " Theresa pulled in a deep breath, trying to regain control of the situation. "It's late and I have to get home."

Ray looked disappointed. "You sure?"

Theresa nodded several times. "Yeah,

thanks for dinner, and, um," — she coughed — "everything."

Ray stuck his hands in his pockets, not sure why the magical mood had changed so quickly. "Well, I — I hope I see you again."

Theresa smiled weakly, deciding to avoid the entire issue. "Good-bye," she said, and walked away.

Timmy ran up to Ray, holding a sparkler, and she turned to look at them together. Timmy waved and Theresa returned the wave before walking swiftly away, torn by conflicting emotions. If she stayed any longer, she wasn't going to be able to make herself leave.

She walked along with her head down, going over every moment of the day and trying to figure out how she could have let things get so out of hand.

Alex stepped out from behind a tree, his arms folded across his chest, blocking her way.

"What're *you* doing here?" she asked, startled.

He looked at her without blinking. "I could ask you the same question."

"I — " She didn't really have an answer. "I'm just doing my job — "

"*Oh*," he said. "Well, they must be teaching some new stuff at the academy, because I didn't think we were allowed to kiss the suspect."

Theresa looked down at her shiny, elegant high heels, groping for an explanation.

"Maybe *I'm* the one getting too involved," Alex said, and paused. "I can't be your partner anymore."

Theresa started to argue, but then just nodded. After her behavior today, she wouldn't want to be her partner, either.

The next morning, Bobbie and Carl were still in the precinct holding cell. They were sharing quarters with a few other prisoners, and Bobbie paced back and forth like a caged cat, scowling at anyone who got near him.

"Ray set us up," he said, for maybe the six-hundredth time. "He and his kid set us up."

Carl ignored that, since he had been hearing it for the last eighteen hours. "When do they feed us in here?"

"We had chili dogs yesterday," one of the other prisoners said.

Carl's face brightened. *"Chili dogs . . ."*

Bobbie grabbed him by the lapels, spinning him around. "Would you quit thinking of food for once!" he said. "We trusted Ray and look where it got us!"

Carl smoothed his jacket, inspecting the seams for any possible minute damage. "Don't get yourself all in a knot, Bob. They got nothing on us except stealing church wine. They're not going to hold us for *that*."

"Yeah, maybe you're right," Bobbie said, calming down a little. "But I'll tell you one thing — when we get out of here, I'm going after that kid." He punched his fist into his other hand for emphasis, then frowned. "And if Ray thinks I'm buying him a new toaster oven — he's *crazy*."

Lieutenant Romayko marched down the hallway of that same precinct house with Theresa at his heels. Continuing with the more feminine look she had had the night before, her hair was free and flowing.

"Who gave you the authority to start

going steady with the suspect?" Lieutenant Romayko demanded.

Theresa sighed. "Sir, I'm sorry, I know I got too close — but I think it's going to pay off. The suspect's son told me he knows something that his father wants him to tell him — but the boy is afraid to tell because that could mean the father would get in trouble."

Lieutenant Romayko stopped, cocking an eyebrow at her. "Do you just make this stuff up, Walsh?" he asked. "Or do you have it written down someplace?"

Doggedly, Theresa plowed on, showing him the treasure map. "The two arrested at the church had this," she said. "They're not talking, but I think it's a treasure map, sir. I think the boy drew it — and he knows where the coins are." She frowned. "I *think*."

Lieutenant Romayko looked at her dubiously, but then eyed the map with interest.

"In that case, the kid's an accessory," he said.

Since she hadn't thought about that,

Theresa's brow furrowed. The *last* thing she wanted to do was get Timmy in trouble.

"Don't let him out of our sight," Lieutenant Romayko said. "That's an order."

Theresa nodded, reluctantly.

At Ray's apartment, Timmy was on the couch, laughing. He had plugged his camcorder into the television and was watching highlights of the videos he'd been taking all week. He had the sound turned off and used the remote control to fast-forward through some parts. He laughed, watching scenes of them all at the aquarium, and then at the baseball game.

In the bathroom, Ray finished brushing his teeth with his new toothbrush and put it into the holder next to Timmy's brush. Somehow, they seemed to belong together there, and he smiled.

He walked out to the hallway, watching the video from a distance. Seeing the shots of him with Timmy, he realized, for the first time, that he really *did* want to have his son in his life.

The phone rang, yanking him out of his

pleasant reverie. He went into the kitchen and picked it up.

"Hello," he said. "Mr. Wankmueller, hi, I was going to call you." He listened. "Rudy called in sick? Aw, he's probably just hung over. . . . Yeah, I know you've got the Thompson wedding, but — " He glanced at Timmy, laughing on the couch. "You're really in a bind? Okay, I could come in for a few hours if it's an emergency. Sure."

Timmy was now watching video from the ice rink, laughing as the camera zoomed in on Bobbie and Carl colliding, and then sprawling on the ice. Something in the background caught his eye, and he pressed the pause button and moved off the couch to get a closer look.

On screen, there was a female figure standing behind the glass at the rink's edge. Timmy stared at her, realizing that it was — *Theresa*.

Ray hung up the phone and came in.

"Listen, Tim, I have to go to work for a few hours," he said. "How about you come with me? You can watch me work."

Timmy blocked the television so Ray

wouldn't see what was on the screen. "Uh, that's okay, Dad. I think I'll stay here."

Ray picked up his car keys from the end table. "You sure?"

"Yeah," Timmy said. "You go ahead. I'll be fine."

Ray shrugged. "Okay. I'll be back around one."

As soon as he was gone, Timmy turned back to the television. The image was a little fuzzy, but it was very definitely Theresa. What was she doing there? They hadn't even *met* yet then! Slowly, he walked over to the window, his mind awhirl.

Something was very wrong.

Chapter 26

Down in the street, Detectives Chapman and Zinn were sitting in their unmarked car. Seeing Ray come outside, they snapped into action.

"He's on the move," Chapman said. "I'll take the father, you stay with the kid."

Zinn nodded.

Standing at the window, Timmy watched as Ray's car pulled away from the curb. Farther up the street, he saw a strange man get out of a car, then the car started up and followed Ray's car. The strange man stood on the sidewalk in plain sight, lighting a cigarette and looking up at the window where Timmy was.

Timmy ducked out of the way, his eyes widening as he suddenly figured out what was going on.

"Cops," he said, almost whispering. He looked back at the television, and the full truth hit him.

Theresa was a cop, too.

"Oh, no," he said, and sank down on the couch. But even though he was upset, his mind was already working, looking for a way out.

If the police were coming after them, he wasn't going to make it easy.

A little while later, Timmy bounced down the front steps of the building, carrying his backpack and wearing a Giants baseball cap and a black Giants windbreaker.

Detective Zinn, watching from an entryway across the street, spoke into his cellular phone. "The boy just left the apartment, carrying his backpack."

"Don't lose him," Lieutenant Romayko

responded. "He may be going to pick up the coins."

"Hey, he's just a kid," Detective Zinn said. "I got him."

After rounding the corner, Timmy peeked back around the side of the building and saw Detective Zinn crossing over to his side of the street. Now knowing for sure that he was being followed, Timmy turned and hurried down the sidewalk.

The chase was on.

He stopped at a street corner, waiting for the "Walk" sign. Glancing over his shoulder, he saw that Detective Zinn was about thirty yards behind him, seemingly window-shopping.

The light turned green, and Timmy started across the street, seeing Detective Zinn confidently stroll after him. The sidewalk was crowded with vendors and passersby, and Timmy nimbly weaved his way in and out among the people as Detective Zinn followed, doing his best to keep up.

A delivery truck was backed up halfway across the sidewalk, blocking the way with unloaded boxes. Without stopping, Timmy used the boxes as steps and vaulted over the obstruction.

When Detective Zinn got there, he had to go around the boxes and truck, falling farther behind and losing sight of Timmy altogether. He quickened his pace, a little out of breath, scouring the streets for his quarry. He saw a cable car halfway up the street and, suspecting that Timmy was on it, he ran up the middle of the street, trying to catch up. Just as he was closing in, a car pulled out from an alleyway in front of him, and he had to stop — or be run over.

Seeing the cable car making a turn around the next corner, Detective Zinn decided to take a short cut, and ran through the alley.

Timmy was, indeed, riding in the cable car, hunched down, out of sight. Once the cable car had gone around the corner, he jumped off and scanned the street, seeing no sign of the cop. He'd lost him! Flushed with the thrill of victory, he pumped the air with his fist.

But as the cable car pulled away, he saw Detective Zinn standing on the curb across the street, leaning forward with his hands on his knees, trying to catch his breath.

Timmy's first impulse was to run, but he kept his cool. He searched his mind for an idea, his heart pounding wildly. There was an entrance to an underground BART subway station nearby and, sensing a way out, he ran down the steps, knowing that the detective was going to be right behind him.

Timmy bought a farecard and fed it into the turnstile and went through. As he hurried down the crowded stairway to the trains, he glanced back and saw that Detective Zinn was getting close. Then he spied his route of escape — the long, slide-like chute between the two staircases. He jumped on and ZOOM! — slid down the long, two-story slide to the bottom, past the startled looks of the people on the stairs.

Detective Zinn had to push his way laboriously past the crowd, losing ground with every step.

Down on the platform, Timmy waited anxiously for the train, looking over his shoulder every few seconds. Standing a few feet away were a boy about his age and two chattering women. Detective Zinn had appeared on the platform now and stopped about twenty feet away. They both stared straight ahead, follower and followee, pretending not to see each other.

The train pulled in, and people started boarding. Timmy got on one of the cars, and the other boy and the two women sat down across from him. Playing it very cool, Timmy pulled a book from his backpack and started to read.

Detective Zinn entered the next car down, went to the end of it, and looked through the window into Timmy's car. He saw Timmy sitting there, quietly reading, and relaxed a little. The kid wouldn't be able to lose him *now*.

Timmy shifted his eyes over the top of his book, planning his move. He looked at the boy across from him and smiled.

The boy smiled back, obviously very bored by being with two women who were jabbering away as though he weren't even there.

The doors closed, and the train started to move.

Detective Zinn turned his back slightly so that Timmy wouldn't see him talking into his cellular phone. "He got on at Montgomery and we're heading west," he said, confident in the knowledge that his prey wasn't going anywhere. In that spirit, he winked at a leggy blonde sitting nearby, who batted her eyes flirtatiously.

The train rumbled along through the tunnel and pulled into the next station. As the doors opened and people got on and off, Detective Zinn looked through the glass, seeing Timmy still in the same place, reading his book.

The doors closed, and the train started moving again. Detective Zinn shot another look at the leggy blonde — and noticed, over her shoulder, Timmy standing on the platform outside, smugly smiling and waving at him!

Panicked, Detective Zinn looked back into Timmy's car and saw that it was the *other* boy wearing the Giants cap and windbreaker.

One of the women with the boy suddenly noticed that he was now sitting across the aisle, wearing a strange cap and wind-breaker.

"Billy, where'd you get that jacket?" she asked.

"A kid gave it to me," the boy said. "Cool, huh?"

Detective Zinn, trapped on the moving train, watched in horror as Timmy escaped down the platform. Then he covered his head with his arms for a few seconds before calling in the bad news.

Lieutenant Romayko was *not* going to be happy.

Out on the platform, Timmy kept running until he had gone all the way up the stairs, through the exit, and two blocks down the street. He stopped on a corner, winded, checking over his shoulder. There was no one in sight, and he smiled, knowing that this time he had lost the cops for sure.

Then he looked across the street and saw the Neiman Marcus department store. Instantly, his smile widened.

He had just come up with the *perfect* plan.

Chapter 27

Lieutenant Romayko was, indeed, not amused when he heard the news.

"You *lost* him?" he barked into the phone as he stood behind the desk in his office. "How could you lose a kid? Get your butt back to the apartment. I want that boy picked up the minute he shows his face!" He slammed the phone down and glared at Theresa, who was standing quietly near the door.

"Sir," she said, sounding tentative. "If we pick the boy up, we might not get anything from him. But if *I* could get him alone, away from Ray — "

"Oh," Lieutenant Romayko nodded grimly, "so it's 'Ray' now."

" — uh, I mean, the suspect," Theresa said, correcting herself smoothly. "I think he might tell me everything."

Lieutenant Romayko fixed her with a stern look, then gave up and popped a vitamin pill. "I keep taking these things, but they sure don't make me any smarter." He looked up, waving her away. "Well, *go*."

Theresa went.

As Timmy headed for the Greyhound bus station, he checked over his shoulder every so often just to make sure that he was still alone. He walked in through the busy front entrance and headed straight for the lockers. He took the blue Nike travel bag out of his backpack, put some quarters in the slot of a locker, slammed the bag inside, and pocketed the key.

Then, looking as though a great weight had been lifted from his shoulders, he walked away from the bank of lockers toward the exit.

So far, the plan was working just fine.

*   *   *

At the bakery, Ray was carefully icing a cake when his boss, Mr. Wankmueller, came up to admire his work.

"How'd that family emergency come out?" Mr. Wankmueller asked. "Everything okay?"

"Yeah, everything's fine," Ray said briefly. Then, realizing that he owed the man more than that, he put down the small spatula he was using and looked right at him. "It was my son. He came to visit, and I needed to spend some time with him."

Mr. Wankmueller smiled understandingly. "That's good, Ray."

Ray nodded. "Yeah. I've been doing some thinking, and — " Spoken aloud, the thoughts would maybe seem more real. "He might be moving in."

"That's nice, Ray," Mr. Wankmueller said with genuine affection in his voice. "I've been doing some thinking, too. If you want to buy the place, it's yours."

Delighted, Ray grabbed his hand, pumping it up and down. "You mean it?" he asked. "That's terrific, Mr. Wankmueller, this is great! I can't tell you how much this means to me — "

One of the other bakers came over to them. "Ray, phone for you," he said.

"Oh." Ray stopped shaking his boss's hand. "Excuse me." He went over to the phone on the wall, expecting to hear his son's voice, but hearing the cynical drawl of the man who was going to fence the coins, instead. "You're early, Dobbs, I wasn't expecting you until tomorrow," he said. "No, no problems, everything's under control. . . . Tonight? Yeah, sure, tonight." He grabbed a floury pen, writing down on a small piece of paper the address where Dobbs wanted them to meet. "Yeah, got it. Fine. See you with the merchandise."

Slowly, he hung up the phone. It was crunch time now — he had to get those coins.

As soon as his replacement showed up, he rushed back home, taking the front steps three at a time. He ran upstairs and burst into the apartment, out of breath.

"Timmy!" he shouted. "Tim, where are you?"

Timmy came out of the bedroom, yawning and looking very innocent. "Hi, Dad," he said. "How was work?"

Ray dismissed that with one wave of his hand, wanting to get right down to business. "Where are the coins, Tim?" he demanded. "I need to know right now."

Timmy moved his jaw, trying to decide what to tell him. "Dad, the police — " He stopped, wondering if he should take a more subtle tack. "What if the police know?"

Ray sucked in his breath, doing his best to keep his anger in check. "Tim, I don't want to have to ask you again — "

"You'd go for the coins *anyway*, wouldn't you," Timmy said with disgust. "You'd try to outsmart them — but you'd get caught."

They locked eyes, fighting a battle of wills. Then Timmy relented.

"Fine, Dad. Have it your way," he said, and went over to the elephant fern in the corner. The plant had perked up a little, showing new life. "I've been watering it," Timmy explained. "Thought it'd be the last place you'd look." He dug into the wet soil, bringing out the key to the bus station locker. "It's in a locker at the bus station."

Relaxing slightly, Ray strode over and plucked the key from his hand. "Thanks, Tim. You came through for me."

Unfortunately, the feeling wasn't mutual. "Sure," Timmy said flatly, and looked around at the disordered room. "Well, I guess I should pack."

Ray looked confused. "Pack?"

Timmy nodded, gathering up his camcorder and videotapes. "I'm going home," he said.

"But — " Ray shook his head, not sure what was happening. "What do you mean, you're going home? I thought you wanted to live here."

"I *do*," Timmy said. "But not if you get the coins."

Now, Ray understood. "What are you saying?" he asked, his fist clenched around the locker key. "I have to choose between you and the coins?"

Timmy thought about that, then nodded. "Well, yeah. Because if you take the coins, you'll never see me again. You'll be in prison. And *this* time, I won't write." He walked past his father and into the bedroom.

"You're *really* making me angry here, Tim," Ray said, going after him. "You have *no* right to make me choose between you and two hundred and fifty grand. It's the biggest break of my life, and I'm not letting it get away from me!"

Timmy didn't answer as he opened his small suitcase across the bed and started packing his clothes.

"Tim!" Ray said sharply.

Timmy didn't even look up.

"Fine!" Ray said. "You want to go, then go! I don't need you!" He stormed back into the living room, his gaze falling upon the rejuvenated plant. Resenting the new life, *and* what it signified, he angrily jerked it free of the soil and tossed it out the open window.

Below him, Theresa was coming up the steps. She was looking very pretty in a bright summery dress. The plant crashed onto the ground beside her, dirt spraying all over her legs. She stopped and looked up at the window, wondering what was going on in there.

She was pretty sure that it wasn't anything good.

It took a few hours, but Bobbie and Carl finally made bail and were released from the San Francisco holding facility. They hustled out of the building, wanting to make up for the day and a half they had lost.

"I told you they wouldn't keep us," Carl said cheerfully, looking up at the bright sunshine and clear blue sky.

"Yeah," Bobbie agreed, looking very grim. "And now that we're out — it's *payback time.*"

Chapter 28

Carl wasn't sure what to say. He was worried about what Bobbie might have in mind.

"Well," he started, "shouldn't we — "

"*First*, we're going to make a little stop," Bobbie said, lifting one arm up as they approached the curb. "Taxi! Hey, taxi!"

A cab swerved to a halt next to them.

"Where we going?" Carl asked uneasily.

"Just get in the cab," Bobbie said, and pushed him inside.

Ray was still standing in the middle of his living room, fuming, when there was a knock on the door. He threw it open, only to see Theresa.

"What?!" he yelled.

Theresa blinked, taken aback by his tone. "Hi. Uh, I saw a plant fly out your window."

He let the door swing open the rest of the way so she could come in.

"It was dead," he said, without much interest.

"Oh." Theresa looked around, then touched her hair self-consciously. "Um, I had a great time last night, Ray, and — "

He walked away from her, making it clear that he wasn't in the mood to talk.

"Um, is Timmy here?" she asked.

"Yeah," Ray said, and jerked his thumb in the direction of the bedroom. "He's here."

Theresa frowned, not exactly overwhelmed by the enthusiasm in his voice. "Well," she said. "It was so nice of him to get me that cologne, and I thought — if it's okay with you," she added hastily, "I'd take him to the movies or something. Just the two of us."

Timmy came out of the bedroom with his

suitcase and backpack, looking just as sullen as his father did.

"He can't go," Ray said shortly. "I'm taking him to the bus station. He's going home."

Theresa shot a glance at Timmy's suitcase, wondering if the coins could be in there. "Oh," she said. "Well. That's too bad."

Ray shrugged, completely expressionless. "And we're kind of pressed for time here."

"Oh." Theresa forced a smile. "Well. Timmy, it was really fun being with you and . . . I hope we can do it again." At a loss for what to do next, she leaned over and gave him an awkward hug.

Since Timmy knew her real motives, he held himself very stiffly, not responding at all.

"Sure," he said, and pulled away, following his father downstairs to the car.

Theresa trailed after them uncertainly.

"Thanks a lot for coming by," Ray said, making sure Timmy was in the car and then closing the door. "But we really have to go."

Watching them leave was tearing her apart inside, and Theresa decided to give Ray one last chance to save himself.

"Ray, wait," she said.

He stopped with his hand on the driver's door.

"Isn't there *any* way I can get you to change your plans?" she asked.

He didn't quite understand the intensity in her voice, but shook his head regardless. "No. I have to go."

As the car pulled away, Theresa waved a little forlornly, but neither of them even glanced back at her.

Down the street, the taxi carrying Bobbie and Carl was just about to stop when they saw Ray driving away.

Bobbie looked at Carl, and then leaned forward to get the driver's attention.

"Follow that car," he said.

Theresa also followed Ray's car, talking into her police radio as she drove.

"They're headed to the Greyhound station," she reported. "He's putting his son on a bus, and the coins should be in the boy's suitcase."

"Okay," Lieutenant Romayko answered. "If the boy gets on the bus with the bag, let him go. We'll pull him off at the first stop."

"Ten-four," Theresa said, and replaced the handset in its holder, deciding to concentrate on her driving instead of the unhappy scene in which she was about to play a major role.

At the bus terminal, Ray and Timmy stood in line at the ticket counter, both with their arms tightly folded across their chests.

"You get on that bus, you're making a big mistake," Ray said in a low voice, staring straight ahead.

Timmy shrugged, his face rigid with determination. "I'm not making the mistake, Dad. *My* bus is going to Redding. *Yours* is headed to Folsom."

"Will you stop with that!" Ray snapped, and then saw that they were next in line. "Last chance. You staying or not?"

"That's up to you," Timmy said stubbornly.

They looked at each other, neither one

of them about to back down, and then Ray turned to the ticket agent.

"One-way ticket to Redding," he said.

After bickering a little about who was going to pay the fare, Bobbie and Carl ran into the bus terminal and scanned the main lobby for Ray and Timmy.

"There they are," Bobbie said, pointing to them as they left the ticket counter. "Come on!"

Carl hung back. "He was buying a ticket. Maybe the kid is leaving."

Bobbie started after them, with nothing but revenge on his mind, but Carl jerked him back.

"*No*," he said. "We talk to him outside. *After* he puts his kid on the bus."

Bobbie didn't want to wait, but Carl's eyes — and hands — were holding him so firmly that he nodded, and they leaned against a nearby wall to wait.

All around the bus terminal, various members of the San Francisco Police Department were coming in, taking up their assigned posts. Theresa concealed herself by pretending to read a newspaper, while her partner Alex entered the lobby through another door. Then Detectives Chapman and Zinn drifted in, trying to look inconspicuous.

This case was about to break wide open.

Ray and Timmy stood uncomfortably in the bus departure area, avoiding each other's eyes. The bus to Redding was about to leave, and Ray lifted Timmy's suitcase into the baggage hold.

"All aboard for Redding!" the announcer called.

It was time to say good-bye, and Ray couldn't quite face it.

"You, uh, you really are a little pain in the neck," he said finally, "you know that?"

Timmy nodded. "Thanks for teaching me about art and how to pick up girls."

Now they looked at each other. Timmy desperately wanted his father to choose him over the coins. Ray wanted his son, but just couldn't bring himself to sacrifice the big score. They were both so strong-willed — like father, like son — that neither of them wanted to be the one to give in.

Timmy let out his breath. "It's okay, Dad," he said. "I don't need a hug." Then he turned abruptly and boarded the bus without looking back.

Ray stood alone on the loading platform and watched his son walk out of his life.

Chapter 29

Unable to watch anymore, Ray walked
back into the station, his mind churning.
What was he supposed to do? He *desperately* needed the money. If Timmy loved
him, he wouldn't expect him to give up the
chance to *be* somebody, for once — right?

He headed for the lockers, unaware of
the many eyes — police and criminal —
that were following his every move. He
glanced down at the key, then located
locker number twenty-five.

He stood in front of it, debating what to
do. If he opened it, he would lose his son;
if he *didn't* open it, he was walking away

from a quarter of a million dollars. Either way, he would be making a big mistake.

Alex and Detective Zinn waited tensely about fifty feet away, ready to take him in.

"It's in a locker," Detective Zinn said.

"Don't make a move until he opens it," Alex reminded him. "Until he *has it in his hands*."

Theresa, who was on the other side of the lobby, watched Ray stand frozen in front of the locker. She was hoping — against all her professional instincts — that he wouldn't open it.

Ray eyed the locker and then the key in his hand.

"You just have to decide," he murmured. "What's more important . . ."

"Bus number ten sixty-five, now leaving for Sacramento, Chico, Red Bluff, and Redding," the terminal announcer said over the loudspeaker. "Last call."

Ray looked at the locker and then sighed wearily.

"I'm going to regret this," he said, and then started running back toward the gate, dodging past people in the crowded lobby. "Excuse me, excuse me, out of my way!"

This sudden flight sent Alex and Detective Zinn into a panic.

"He's made us," Detective Zinn said. "Let's take him."

Alex shook his head in frustration. "Probable cause. We can't. He's *got* to open the locker." He caught Theresa's eye and motioned for her to stay where she was.

In the bus departure area, the bus door closed, and the bus slowly started to pull out.

Ray ran in front of it, signalling "STOP!" by waving both arms.

The driver jammed on the brakes and opened the door. "What do you want?" he asked, annoyed.

"My son," Ray said, and took the steps in two jumps. He looked around until he located Timmy about ten seats away. "Let's get one thing straight, okay?" he said to him from the front of the bus. "We're going to have to change the living arrangements, because I'm *not* sleeping on that couch every night."

Timmy broke into a wide smile and ran up the aisle to him. He stopped just short of his father and looked at him tentatively.

Ray stepped forward and took him into his arms, giving Timmy the hug he'd wanted for years. Timmy hugged back, happier than he could ever remember being.

They retrieved his suitcase from the baggage hold and walked back into the station.

"How about if we move?" Timmy suggested. "We can get a two-bedroom place."

"Oh, sure, like I can afford that now," Ray said, grinning wryly.

They were passing the lockers, and he gave locker number twenty-five a wistful look.

"What if I just took *some* of the coins," he said. "You know, five or six, just for expenses — "

Timmy just looked at him.

"Fine," Ray said, recognizing a lost cause when he saw one. "So I don't buy the bakery."

"So we'll save our money," Timmy said cheerfully. "You'll get it someday."

Bobbie, standing with Carl, couldn't hold himself back any longer.

"I'm getting him now," he said.

Carl brusquely grabbed his arm and yanked him back.

"Hey, if you're not with me, I'll do this myself!" Bobbie said, jerking loose and stalking off.

Carl stayed right where he was, wanting no part of that.

"Come on, Dad," Timmy said, eager to leave the locker area once and for all. "Let's get out of here."

"Not so fast," a familiar surly voice said behind them.

They turned and saw Bobbie.

"Open the locker," he said, and lifted his coat, revealing his gun underneath. "Open it, Ray. And give me the coins. I know they're in there."

Ray shook his head. "Aw, Bob, put that away. You know you're not going to do anything with it."

Bobbie's shoulders slumped, his bluff called. "You *never* take me seriously," he said, then grabbed the gun and pointed it at Ray, his hand shaking. "But you're taking me seriously now, Ray. Open the locker!"

Seeing that he meant business, Ray raised his hands enough to show that he was no threat.

"All right, Bob," he said, taking the key from his pocket. "Okay, I'm doing it." He inserted it in the keyhole and opened the locker, revealing the bag. As he lifted it from the locker, Bobbie smiled and reached out to claim it.

"Freeze!" Alex yelled, with his gun drawn.

They turned to see Alex, and Detectives Chapman and Zinn upon them. Bobbie tried to run, but Detective Chapman disarmed him and then slapped on a pair of handcuffs.

"Ray Gleason, Bobbie Drace, you're under arrest," Alex said in a deep voice. He clamped handcuffs onto a surprised Ray as Detective Zinn grabbed the blue Nike bag.

Ray submitted mutely, making no effort to resist.

Carl, standing near the exit doors, shook his head sadly. It was over, and all he could do now was try to avoid getting caught himself. He made sure that no one was looking at him and then slipped out the door to freedom.

"You have the right to remain silent," Alex said, reading Ray and Bobbie their Miranda rights. "Anything you say can and will be used against you — "

"Dad, what's going on?" Timmy asked, his eyes wide.

Ray gave him a defeated shrug. "I think somebody's made a big mistake, Tim."

"Yeah!" Bobbie agreed. "I haven't done nothing!"

Theresa joined the group, looking guilty.

"Theresa," Ray said, more than a little surprised to see her.

"I'm sorry, Ray," she said, unable to meet his eyes. "I'm really sorry."

Detective Zinn unzipped the Nike bag to make sure that all of the coins were there. He looked inside, blinked, and looked again. The bag was full of coins, but they weren't rare — or valuable.

The bag was full of hundreds and hundreds of *pennies*.

Chapter 30

The whole group travelled back to the precinct house in several cars, in complete silence. Once they got there, Detective Zinn, Alex, Theresa, and Lieutenant Romayko gathered in a small room to examine their nonexistent evidence.

Detective Zinn overturned the travel bag on an empty table, and the hundreds of pennies spilled out.

"All of them pennies," he said grimly. "And believe me, none of them worth more than one cent."

Alex nodded, just as grim. "The kid's

suitcase was clean, too. So was Gleason's car and apartment."

"Well," Lieutenant Romayko said, sounding calm and *looking* furious. "There's only one thing to do, then." He paused. "Let's break out the floppy shoes and funny noses *because we sure do look like clowns!*"

The rest of them agreed.

A few minutes later, Theresa brought Timmy into an interrogation room, and they sat down across from each other at a scarred wooden table.

"Okay," Theresa said, struggling to sound official. "Now, you say you put the pennies in the bag and put it in the locker."

"Uh-huh," Timmy said, nodding ingenuously. "Is that against the law?"

"No," Theresa said, fighting simultaneous urges to laugh — and yell — at him. "But why did you do it?"

Timmy shrugged. "I won the pennies playing poker, and I didn't want them stolen."

Theresa looked at him, then leaned forward, folding her hands. "You know I'm your friend, Timmy," she started.

He nodded. "I know. Want to come for dinner tonight?"

"Timmy, this is a very serious matter," she said, looking at him intensely. "Over a million dollars in coins have been stolen, and I want you tell me everything you know about the robbery."

Timmy pondered this for a minute, then looked up. "Do you have a boyfriend?"

Theresa sighed and rubbed her temples with one hand. "Timmy — "

"I'm just asking a question," he said defensively. "I thought we were friends."

Theresa moved her jaw, feeling trapped by her own words. "No. I don't have a boyfriend," she said.

"You must be pretty lonely, huh?" Timmy asked.

Theresa sighed again. Clearly, the only thing she was going to get out of this conversation was a headache.

"I was like that after my mom died," Timmy said. "It hurt a lot and I never thought it'd go away. But now I got my dad back and — " He smiled weakly. "I'm still going to miss her. But I think it's going to be okay."

Theresa nodded. She realized that he was never going to tell her anything about what happened.

"*And*," Timmy said, "I know whoever stole those coins is real sorry they did it, and they'll never steal anything again."

Theresa nodded stiffly. "That's wonderful, Tim. But the coins are still missing. Could you 'guess' where they might be?"

Timmy shrugged. "I don't know. They could be in a bag, maybe."

"You mean — like the bag you put the pennies in?" Theresa asked, carefully leading him.

"Yeah," Timmy agreed. "And maybe people could walk past it and not even know it's there. Maybe the guy *holding* it doesn't even know." Then, he grinned at her.

Theresa sat back, chewing on this, well aware he had just given her everything she needed. All she had to do was figure it out.

The answer was at Neiman Marcus. Theresa retraced their steps from the day before, and when she walked into the men's department, she saw it.

Standing stiffly posed in sporting clothes

was the mannequin they had passed — and it still had an *identical blue Nike bag* slung over its shoulder.

Theresa looked at the mannequin and smiled.

Maybe she was a better investigator than she thought.

Carl was sitting at a lunch counter, eating a chili dog, when the news broke on television.

"A startling development in the recent one million dollar rare coin robbery happened today," the anchorperson announced. "A tip given to the police resulted in the recovery of the entire cache of stolen coins. Oddly enough, the coins were found in a small travel bag that was hanging on a mannequin in the men's department in Neiman Marcus department store."

Carl, about to take a bite of chili dog, reacted to the news, and some chili dripped onto his tie. He looked up at the television, and then down at his tie.

"Darn," he said, and dipped his napkin into his water glass so he could scrub the spot off.

*   *   *

The television was also on in Lieutenant Romayko's office, and he and Theresa were watching the report.

"The robbery is still under investigation," the anchorperson was saying, "but the San Francisco police have yet to arrest any suspects in the case."

Lieutenant Romayko turned off the television and grabbed a bottle of vitamins from his desk.

"And we won't, either," he said as he shook his head, and looked at Theresa. "Well, we got the coins back, at least."

Theresa nodded.

"And, under the circumstances, you did okay, Walsh," he said grudgingly. "You're off probation. You might make it here, after all."

Theresa smiled, glowing in the praise. "Thank you, sir." Then, seeing that he couldn't open the vitamin bottle, she took it, effortlessly twisted off the lid, and gave it back to him.

Lieutenant Romayko lifted an eyebrow at her. "Don't get cocky, Walsh," he said.

She grinned at him.

*   *   *

The police had no reason to hold them, so Ray and Timmy were released.

"Let's go home, Dad," Timmy said.

As Ray started to nod, he saw Theresa across the lobby. She hesitated, and then came over, the two of them holding a long look. If she wasn't a cop, and he wasn't an ex-con . . .

"It's like what I said about cops," Ray said with a shrug. "They assume too much. Some things aren't always what they seem."

"And sometimes they are," Theresa said wryly, "but you just can't prove it."

They both nodded, and there was an awkward silence.

"So, you coming to dinner tonight?" Timmy asked.

Theresa looked at him, not sure what to say, so Ray said it for her.

"Maybe some other time, Tim," he said. "You see, there's this thing about cops and ex-cons. There's kind of an official waiting period between the time they arrest you and the time you can ask one out."

Theresa smiled at that. "Take care of

him," she said to Ray, indicating Timmy.

"I will," Timmy said, and they all laughed.

Theresa watched them walk away — and then watched her partner Alex watching *her*.

"You're spying on me again, Ceranski," she said.

He nodded. "I know. I have to stop doing that."

"Yeah," she said, then looked at him thoughtfully. "So. You busy tonight? You maybe want to get some dinner?"

"I don't think so," he said, and caught Detective MacReady's eye from across the room. "I kind of have a date with MacReady. I think she's more my type."

Theresa looked over at Detective MacReady and smiled. "That's good," she said. "I think so, too."

Outside, Ray and Timmy walked down the steps to the street.

"Wait until I get you home," Ray said. "You *knew* the cops were watching and you didn't tell me!"

Timmy shrugged. "Because you

would've tried to outsmart them and gotten caught. So while no one was looking, I took the bag and switched it for the one on the mannequin. And put *that* one in the locker."

"Yeah, but you let me *open* the locker and get arrested," Ray said.

Timmy nodded solemnly. "I guess you learned a lesson, huh?"

"Yeah," Ray said. "*Never* have children."

Timmy laughed. "Admit it, Dad. If it wasn't for me, you'd be rotting in stir."

"Hey," Ray said, shrugging. "At least I'd have a bed to sleep in."

They kept walking down the street, heading in no particular direction, for no particular reason.

"So, what do you want to do now, Dad?" Timmy asked.

"Well, I just lost a quarter million bucks and gained a permanent house guest." Ray thought for a second. "How about I go drown myself."

How long was "an official waiting period"? Timmy couldn't wait to find out.

"How about we go shoot hoops and pick up girls?" Timmy suggested.

"We could do that, too," Ray said, and slung his arm around his son's shoulder.

Timmy grinned. He had now gotten what he had always wanted.

So far, it had been the greatest week of his entire life.

10